Will's
viewpoint

"Your drawings of the body weren't right."

Still speechless from his story, I could only shrug. The busboy came by and asked for our dirty dishes. We both signaled that he could take them away.

"I should get back to work," I said when the table was clear.

"She wasn't curled up like you had her in the drawings."

"Will, please. Maybe the whole thing is something we should be forgetting."

He stretched out his arms. "It was like she was lunging for something or had jumped and crashed. She was coated in ice, even her face was covered. That's how I knew she was dead." He swore softly. "One minute I'm running along and thinking about the cinnamon rolls my grandpa was putting in the oven when I left the house and then the next thing I'm doing is looking at a dead girl."

"There was nothing about you on the news, just that an unidentified jogger had found the body."

He shrugged. "I'm a minor." His eyes met mine for the first time since he'd described her body. "If you're not eighteen, they can't . . . Oh, Hanna, it's sort of complicated."

I picked up my purse and rose from the table. "I'm off work at eight. Can you hang around?" He nodded. I hugged him. "Meet me in the bookstore across the street."

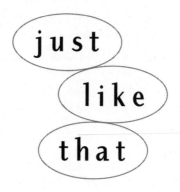

just like that

marsha qualey

speak
An Imprint of Penguin Group (USA) Inc.

SPEAK
Published by the Penguin Group
Penguin Group (USA), Inc., 345 Hudson Street, New York, New York 10014, U.S.A.
Penguin Group (Canada), 90 Eglinton Avenue East, Suite 700,
Toronto, Ontario, Canada M4P 2Y3 (a division of Pearson Penguin Canada Inc.)
Penguin Books Ltd, 80 Strand, London WC2R 0RL, England
Penguin Ireland, 25 St Stephen's Green, Dublin 2, Ireland (a division of Penguin Books Ltd)
Penguin Group (Australia), 250 Camberwell Road, Camberwell, Victoria 3124, Australia
(a division of Pearson Australia Group Pty Ltd)
Penguin Books India Pvt Ltd, 11 Community Centre,
Panchsheel Park, New Delhi - 110 017, India
Penguin Group (NZ), 67 Apollo Drive, Rosedale, North Shore 0745, Auckland, New Zealand
(a division of Pearson New Zealand Ltd)
Penguin Books (South Africa) (Pty) Ltd, 24 Sturdee Avenue,
Rosebank, Johannesburg 2196, South Africa

Registered Offices: Penguin Books Ltd, 80 Strand, London WC2R 0RL, England

First published in the United States of America by Dial Books,
a member of Penguin Group (USA) Inc., 2005
Published by Speak, an imprint of Penguin Group (USA), Inc., 2007

9 10

Copyright © Marsha Qualey, 2005
All rights reserved

Text set in Hoefler Text
Designed by Nancy R. Leo-Kelly

THE LIBRARY OF CONGRESS HAS CATALOGED THE DIAL EDITION AS FOLLOWS:
Qualey, Marsha.
Just like that / Marsha Qualey.
p. cm.
Summary: A tragic accident ending with the death of two people her own age changes life
forever for an eighteen-year-old woman.
ISBN: 0-8037-2840-9 (hc)
[1. Grief—Fiction. 2. Accidents—Fiction. 3. Friendship—Fiction. 4. Family life—Fiction.
5. Interpersonal relationships—Fiction. 6. Dating (Social customs)—Fiction.]
I. Title.
PZ7.Q17Ju 2005 [Fic]—dc22 2004024177

Speak ISBN 978-0-14-240830-8

Text set in Hoefler Text
Designed by Nancy R. Leo-Kelly

Printed in the United States of America

For Dave

just like that

1
It Began This Way

I suspect that sometimes strangers think I'm a bitch. I can't say for sure, though, because I never ask strangers what they think.

My friend Maura does. If we're having an argument on the bus, say, and she wants support for her side, she'll turn to anyone who may have heard us and she'll ask what they think about it all. We could be discussing politics, CDs, makeup—anything. Once on the 6B when we were headed home after seeing a movie, she turned to the woman sitting next to her and asked, "Don't you think using tampons can be bad for your health?"

Kelsey was sitting next to me in the seats facing Maura and the woman. She made a weird low noise that was shaped out of Maura's name: *Mor-uuuuuh.*

I just waited and watched. What happens next? I always want to know that.

The woman shifted the plastic shopping bags on her lap. One sagged, and a can of Pounce cat treats almost fell out. She narrowed her eyes and said, "No. Thank god for them, I say. You have no idea what we went through before. Of course, I'm way past needing any of that sort of thing, but it's what I tell my granddaughters. You have no idea, I tell them." She looked down and prodded the Pounce back into the bag, then jerked her head and said, "I need to get off. Pull the stop, please."

I reached for the cord. When my arm shot up, the lady stiffened, as if she had only just then noticed me. She rose and walked toward the front of the bus, throwing me a sharp look as she passed. I'm five ten, but when I'm with Maura or Kelsey, people often don't notice me right away. Why would they? Kels is drop-dead, attention-grabbing gorgeous, while Maura is simply the friendliest person in Minneapolis and is always quick to engage people in conversation. I'm not by nature a quiet person, but when those two start making things happen, I'm happy to turn invisible, sit back, and watch the scene unfold. Weird thing is, when people do realize I'm there and that they've been observed, they get upset. Like a quick change in the weather, their surprise turns to judgment, and suddenly I'm pretty certain that a complete stranger is thinking, Bitch.

→←

"Bitch."

This time I deserved it. After all, no one likes getting dumped. I reached out and tried to take Spencer's hand. I still wanted to be friends.

He flopped back hard against the booth seat. "Please don't look at me like that."

"Like how?"

"Like you're studying me and getting ready to draw what you see."

"I'm not."

"You will." He moved the mug from my paper place mat. There was a perfect brown ring where coffee had soaked through, but otherwise it was blank and inviting. "Go on, draw something. You know you want to."

I didn't move, except for fingers tapping on my thigh.

Spencer clasped his hands together, prayer-like, and leaned on the table. With his neatly trimmed and combed blond hair, light blue shirt, and navy sweater he looked like an earnest off-duty youth pastor. "Do you know how many of your toss-off place mat sketches I've taken with me and taped up in my bedroom? I bet I've got a couple dozen. They could make a book: *Hanna Martin's Complete Guide to Diner Weirdos.* I even took a few with me to school and put them up in my dorm room. If you'd ever visited, you'd know that. Now you'll never visit."

True.

Spencer's good about a lot of things and maybe the best is that he always takes me at my word. So when I say, "I want to break up," he knows I mean it and doesn't try to talk me out of it, though he vents and fumes.

His eyes glazed over and once again he whispered, "Bitch."

It's a funny word to say when you look like you're praying.

→←

He put his arm around me as we left the diner. Breakup etiquette? I wouldn't know. Spencer was my first boyfriend and I'd never done this before. I did know it was better than tears or yelling.

All night it had been snowing the light powdery stuff

that piles up neatly. We used our arms and mittened hands to clear the windshield and windows of his car. "Why?" he said as he unlocked the passenger door for me. It was the first thing he'd said since the second time he called me a bitch. We'd sat for ten, fifteen minutes after that—him seeming to pray, me drawing (you win, Spencer), and neither of us saying a word until I said, "Let's go."

We sat in the car and waited for the air blasting from the vents to turn warm. "We've been together eleven months," I said. "It's more like a habit than a relationship."

"A habit?" He choked out the words, then banged his head against the steering wheel.

This wasn't going well. "Please take me home," I said.

He skidded through the first three intersections, which wasn't like Spencer at all. Mr. Calm, Mr. Reliable, Mr. Steady. Come to think of it, calling me a bitch wasn't like him either.

"It's because of the sex, isn't it?" he said. "You're having regrets that we finally did it when I was home over fall break."

Well, I thought, maybe because of the *dull* sex. The are-we-ready? and talk-it-over-to-death sex we'd discussed in e-mails for weeks before it happened. I cleared my throat and said, "No, Spence. No regrets."

"Then it's got to be Maura. She's probably poisoned you against me. I know she hates me."

"It's not Maura. It's all me."

"But I bet you've talked about this with her and Kelsey. I hate the way you three share everything. A guy can't breathe without you all discussing it."

Why not be honest? He'd survive. "Something has been bugging me for a while, Spence, but I didn't know what it was until I was waiting with your parents at the airport today. I saw all these couples greeting each other and I realized I didn't feel the way they seemed to. After eleven months together, that's how I should feel about you but I don't. I just feel cold. Then it hit me: Break up. Once I let that thought in, everything seemed so right and clear. That's it, Spence. No other reason at all. And Maura and Kelsey have no idea I'm doing this."

He hit the curb in front of my house, which was a good thing because it slowed him down enough to avoid rear-ending a parked car.

As I walked toward the house I heard the whir of his window going down. He shouted, "I was happy about seeing you."

>‹

I taped a note on the fridge for my mother: *Broke up with Spencer. Make sure I'm awake by ten.*

Ten a.m. My mother's worried face kicked off my day. As soon as I was out of the shower and dressed, she started hovering, following me from bathroom to bedroom and back.

"What?" I shouted, turning off the blow-dryer.

She crossed her arms as she leaned against the door frame. "Do you want to talk about it?" She's a small wiry thing, a trained dancer who's in really good shape even at fifty. You could describe her as petite (a word you'd never use for me), but right now she seemed to fill the doorway.

Her interest was my own fault, of course; I'd left the note. "I'm fine."

"Whose idea?"

"Mine."

As she thought about that, I resumed drying my hair, making sure she got blasted every now and then until she finally walked away.

Mom had always liked Spencer. He'd been a student of hers at Whipple Collegiate, the star of three of her shows by the time he graduated. I knew she'd miss the movie star smile at the front door, chatting with him when he came by to pick me up, and his bad jokes.

I'd miss . . . ?

⋟⋞

On the bus to work I pulled out my phone. The lady next to me stiffened and made a throaty sound, obviously a cell phone fascist. "Don't worry," I said to her as I punched Maura's number. "My friends sleep late and I'm just leaving messages." She moved to a different seat.

Kelsey was the first to call back. She used to work at the store (children's department—no one lasts long there), so she can guess when I'm on break and that's when she calls. Maura never thinks about it, so with her sometimes it's day-long phone tag when I'm at work, even if I've told her when to call.

Kelsey was silent for a long time, then she said, "I'm kind of surprised. I know you weren't exactly head over heels, Hanna, but I also know how he feels about you, and, besides, you two made such a great couple."

Which irritated me. Like I'd stick with someone because of how he feels or just because we made a cute couple?

When I finally connected with Maura, she cried, "I knew it was coming!"

Which also irritated me. Like she knew better than me—before me—about things I might do?

I'm kind of surprised.

I knew it was coming!

How weird was that? My two best friends see two entirely different pictures when each looked at me.

⤞⤝

Who buys swimsuits in December?

Women on their way to warm places for Christmas.

Women who buy swimsuits in winter are fearless. Most of them don't hesitate to come out of the dressing room and walk around with the suit on. They stand there barely dressed as they flip through the racks looking for a different size or color or style or maybe a cover-up. And it's not just the skinny ones who join the parade.

I've worked at the store six months. I've seen it all.

Today I kept my smile fresh. When customers asked for my opinion, I said all the right things:

You can machine wash that suit and it won't lose its stretch.

That style doesn't ride up and pinch.

The color looks good on you. Not everyone can wear orange.

After only three hours I'd sold two thousand dollars worth of stuff—my best afternoon ever.

I was ringing up another sale and trying to catch my boss's eye to get the okay for a break when I heard familiar voices giggling near one of the three-way mirrors.

Maura pirouetted in front of her multiple reflections.

She wore an old lady's swimsuit: fat shoulder straps, inflexible cone-shaped cups, pleated skirt.

I finished with my customer, got the nod from the manager, closed the register, and walked over to my friends.

"Good color," I said. "Not everyone can wear that bright a purple." I turned to Kels. "Couldn't you stop her?"

"And when has that been possible?"

"When do you go on break?" Maura asked as she walked toward the dressing room. "We thought we'd cheer you up and buy you supper."

"I don't need cheering up."

Kelsey reached into her bag. "Fine," she said. "Then we'll skip supper and go straight to dessert."

I took the white box she held. "Turtle Bakery!" I opened the container and sighed happily when I saw the layers of chocolate, fudge frosting, and nuts. "Opera cake."

Kelsey held up a plastic bag. "And three forks."

>‹

We went to the Crystal Court of the IDS tower, which is sort of like a town square for downtown Minneapolis, and sat on one of the benches. No one mentioned Spence until we'd finished the cake. Priorities.

Maura finally raised the subject. She tossed her napkin toward a trash can, missed, and rose from the bench to pick it up. "What did he say when you did it?" she asked as she sat back down.

"Called me a bitch."

"He did not!" said Kelsey.

I nodded. "Old Spence was pretty shocked." I replayed

the breakup for them. When I finished the story Kelsey mumbled something, then walked away, disappearing down a corridor of small shops.

"What's with her?" I said.

"Needs her coffee fix, I suppose. It's been at least two hours." Maura slipped her arm through mine. "Kels feels bad for you," she said after a moment. "So do I."

"Funny about that, because I feel really good."

"It might hit you later. Should we hang around and go to Brian's together?"

"Why Brian's?"

"His birthday party, Hanna, remember? I should be there now helping him get ready."

I groaned. "I totally spaced. Maura, he's your boyfriend and I love him, but I definitely don't feel like a party tonight."

"Uh-huh. But you say you feel really good."

"I'm fine."

We stretched our legs out and slumped down on the bench, silently watching the Saturday night parade through the Crystal Court until Maura pointed and said, "*They're* not fine. Either they're on a really bad first date or they're headed straight for a breakup."

A man and a woman, dressed fashionably for a Saturday night on the town, walked slowly across the court. They veered sharply from each other when their hands briefly touched.

Maura pointed in a different direction. "But those two," she whispered, "are a different story. Look how he's patting his jacket pocket. I bet he's got a diamond in there and he can't wait to propose."

"Or he's got cigarettes and he can't wait to get outside."

Maura elbowed me. "You are so heartless sometimes. Hey, here she comes."

Kelsey walked toward us, carrying a green bundle, which she handed to me as she sat down.

"First cake and now flowers?" I folded back the florist's paper: fat pink roses.

"Take care of them," Kelsey ordered.

"How insulting; of course I will. Why do you even say that?"

"Because she knows you," Maura answered. "You'll be headed home and you'll start thinking about something you want to draw and you'll get distracted and leave them on the bus."

"I will not. Kels, this is so sweet. You didn't have to do this."

"I know, but I'm sorry about the way I reacted on the phone this afternoon. With Spence out of the picture you probably won't be getting flowers anymore, so . . ." She shrugged.

"With Spence *in* the picture I never got flowers. Not once."

She was shocked. "You're kidding."

I shook my head. "Why so surprised?"

She looked down. "I guess I just assumed that was his style. It's not Zak's, that's for sure."

"Or Brian's," Maura quickly added. "We certainly picked special ones, didn't we? I say from here on out breakups mean flowers."

I nodded. "We'll make it a rule."

>←

When I got back to the store, the ladies I worked with made a big fuss over the roses and an even bigger fuss over the news that I'd broken up with Spencer.

"It was my idea," I said, "and my heart's not broken."

They made one loud noise. Suddenly I was glad I didn't have an evening filled with Spencer or friends because suddenly I wanted desperately to go home and draw what I saw: three middle-aged mothers playacting Munch's *The Scream*.

><

The house was empty, as I knew it would be. Mom and Charles were out dancing, their usual Saturday night fun.

Six years ago my dad died on the dance floor in the middle of a mambo, slipping out of Mom's arms as he succumbed on the spot to a heart attack.

I like Charles. I like that he knows how my dad died but he's still game.

I reheated leftover chicken and went to my room. I looked out the window as I ate in the dark.

Christmas lights on most of the houses. Car lights moving slowly up and down streets. Black shadows walking on sidewalks. A dog peeing in the snow, then pawing at a door: Let me in, let me in.

Me to Spencer: Let me out.

><

I always swore that I wouldn't give in to the unwritten high school rule that two is the magic number. I swore that I would not feel unformed and less than whole without a mate. Swore that *my* name would not become half of a familiar phrase that had *N* in the middle. Maura-N-

Brian. Kelsey-N-Zak. Jarod-N-Lissa. D'Neeka-N-Cate (though Cate is not totally out yet, so maybe I should leave those two off a list).

Hanna-N-Spence. There it was, almost before I knew something was happening.

I'd known him for years. He was one of the Whipple students I couldn't avoid when I'd show up there to get a ride home with Mom or help out with a play. My mother is the head of the award-winning drama department at the most elite private school in Minneapolis, Minnesota. Her students love her. Last January one of them decided he loved me.

I go to public school. My choice. To hell with the faculty kids' tuition discount at Whipple, the prep school's absence of security guards and metal detectors, its lakeshore campus and college-caliber academics. I like the crush and rush of Humphrey High. I like going to school with kids who've been in this country only a year or two, sometimes less, and—mostly—I like the feeling that anything, *anything*, could happen next.

But damned if I didn't respond when one of the most golden of the golden boys at Whipple turned his sweet steady gaze on me.

A girl could hate herself for such weakness.

÷<

When Maura and Kelsey went through breakups last year it meant hours of temper and tears and long, long talks.

So why didn't I feel worse? But then, wasn't that why I broke it off—because I didn't feel at all?

I stared at the empty street in front of the house, half-expecting to see his car pull up and park. What I did not know as I sat watching in the dark was that after eleven months of comfortable coupledom Spence and I would never physically cross paths again, and that this twenty-four-hour obsession with the breakup would soon pass. In just a few hours its only importance would be that it was the reason behind my decision to quit moping, get up, get out, and take a midnight walk. A walk that changed everything.

2
Thin Ice

Near the top of any girl's list of dumb things to do would be "Take a walk by yourself late at night." It's usually near the top of mine, but sometimes you don't stop to check the list. You just go—out the door and into a cold that socks you right in the face.

After midnight, ten below zero—okay, maybe a solitary walk around the lake wasn't so risky. After all, who was afoot to give me trouble?

As soon as I got to Lake Calhoun I knew I'd never make it all the way around. The wind was too stiff and cold. I sat on a bench by the playground. The moon was high overhead, the pale flat disk an underpowered spot-light on the nocturnal landscape.

One of the apartment buildings on the western shore of the lake was outlined with red and green lights. Holiday lights and holiday cheer. Christmas was in three days. Mom and I would celebrate in our usual fashion: a quick gift exchange, a high-calorie brunch, a movie.

Two shadows on the lake grew closer and larger. Their legs and arms moved in the telltale skier's kick, swing, and glide. I attempted a feeble disappearing act by sinking into the corner of the bench, though I doubted that late-night skiers were any threat to me.

They landed on shore in a burst of laughter. Two women. After they took off their skis, they fell to the ground, and soon I heard sweeter, more intimate sounds. Holy crap, it was below zero—please tell me they wouldn't go at it here.

Making a preemptive strike, I called out, "How was the skiing?"

They both shot to their feet and twisted this way and that—two jerky shadows, two dancing robots. I had to laugh, which I found out immediately was the wrong reaction because one of them came over to the bench. "Is there a problem?" she said. "Have I missed a joke?"

Oh, what crazy thing was this. I take a walk to ponder my cold heart and suddenly I've laughed my way to the edge of a late-night brawl with some chick. "No problem at all," I said. "Sorry to bother you." I pulled up the hood of my parka and tried again to disappear.

Skier Two came over. "Are you okay? Should you be out here by yourself?"

Yes and no. "I'm fine, thanks."

There was a very long silence as they looked at each other and telegraphed some sort of best friend/girlfriend message. Skier Two sat down beside me. The heat of her concerned stare lasered through my parka hood, and I was compelled to turn and give her a carefree smile. No go. She took my fat mittened hand and said, "We're going to Dunn Bros. Come with us. I'd like to buy you a hot chocolate."

Okay, she was worried, so it would take more than a smile to send them away. "Funny you should mention that," I said. "I used to ski the lakes with my dad." Wow. Hadn't thought about that in a long time. "My mom would drop us off at Cedar and we'd end up here and then break out the thermos of cocoa." I pulled my hand from hers. "Thanks for the offer, but no. How was the skiing?"

Skier Two said, "Nice."

One said, "Slow. We didn't wax right, and the ice is tricky. You weren't thinking of going out there, were you? Even with this cold snap it's still thin in spots, and the warning signs aren't all that obvious."

"I'm not going anywhere until I go home," I said, "and home is only a few blocks away, and I'm fine."

"We could walk you," Two said.

"Leave her alone," One growled. "Let's go."

Two stood up. "I'd feel better if we walked her home," she snapped.

I pushed back my hood and faced her just as headlights from a passing car brushed over us. We all looked up the bank to the road. The car braked for a turn and its tail-lights brightened and sprayed red across the snow. "That's beautiful," I said. One and Two turned and looked at me. "I draw and paint. I'm pretty good, but I have no idea how I'd draw what I just saw."

One said, "Then go home and try to figure it out, otherwise she'll never let me leave."

I pulled up my hood. "Pretty soon. I'm going to sit here a bit more. Good night."

One gathered their equipment and walked away. After a moment Two sighed and followed. As they trudged up the steps to the street I shouted, "Please don't have a fight because of me."

They would, of course. You could practically smell the warning musk in the frigid air. No doubt about it: I'd poisoned their happy evening.

Within minutes the silence and my solitude were again disturbed when I heard the roar of an engine. Snowmobiles and ATVs were illegal in the city parks, but that didn't ever stop people from tearing down streets and over the lakes when there was fresh snow. A sinewy cloud of warm breath shot out of my mouth as I swore at the disturbance.

I stood up, ready to stalk away so I could be alone with my bad mood. A four-wheeler raced past me toward the lake. Its bright headlight cut a swath out of the darkness. There were two people on the vehicle. More happy lovers, no doubt. I'd ventured out tonight to purge my head of thoughts of romance and look what I'd run into.

The ATV sped over a snowbank at the edge of the ice and rode the air for a few feet. When it landed, the passenger tumbled off. The driver immediately cut the engine. A girl laughed and shouted, "I love you, Derek!"

I sat back down. The movement must have caught her eye because she called out, "Friend or foe?" They laughed at her wit in a merry tenor-soprano duet. Before I could answer "Foe," they sped off again. Then they made a sharp turn and came toward me, angling away at the last minute and stopping with a spray of snow that missed me by inches. "It's our one-year anniversary!" the girl said. "Here's a present in reverse! Find someone and have fun!" An unwrapped condom landed on my lap.

Sometimes other people's happiness is contagious.

Most times, I suddenly realized, it just sucks. I'd been about to share Skier One's warning about sketchy lake ice, but the girl's giggling as I tossed the condom into a trash can chilled my goodwill. By the time I looked up, the four-wheeler was speeding away. When it was a few yards out, it once again made a sharp turn and came toward me. They circled me a few times, drawing closer with each revolution and pinning me in place. This didn't improve my mood.

The girl's mood had soured too. She pounded the driver's shoulder. "Would you stop it when I tell you to stop it?" she said angrily when the machine finally came to a halt. The boy said something I couldn't hear. She pounded his shoulder again. "Don't make fun of me when I get scared." She got off and walked toward me as he revved the engine and drove away. "I apologize for the moron I'm with," she said. "I guess he was trying to impress you. We're not from this neighborhood, but we know that there's supposed to be an all-night diner nearby. Do you know where it is?"

I pointed across the lake. "A couple of blocks behind the high-rise with the twinkling lights."

The moron returned, stopping the ATV right behind the girl. She set her lips, looked at me, and made a face as he revved the engine. She got back on, pounded his shoulder and shouted, "It's across the lake. Don't drive like an asshole." Within minutes they were way out on the ice and the moron was making tight figure eights.

With not even a wave of a magic wand I'd ruined the night for two happy couples.

Go, Hanna. Cupid's evil twin.

->-<-

Mom and I have got this deal for Sundays. Six days a week we each work and play long hours, but on the seventh day we shut out the rest of the world and catch up. My bosses know I'll work holidays and Friday or Saturday nights with no complaint as long as they never schedule me for Sundays. Her students and colleagues know it's the one day she won't answer the phone. No friends, no boyfriends, no work, no errands. We read, eat, talk, and watch what we've stored up on TiVo.

Sometimes we work together on her shows. I've done the initial design work for the last five plays at Whipple. Mom will tell me how she pictures the stage in her head, how she wants her actors to move and look amid the scenery, and I start drawing.

This winter's show was going to be *Our Town*. I groaned when she told me. "I can't believe Dean Stratford is happy you're doing something so familiar and ordinary."

"We'll breathe new life into it." She handed me a mug of hot cider. "I should have done it last year. Spence would have made a dreamy George. So sweet and earnest." She cradled her mug. "Oops."

I picked up the script. "Don't worry about me. Like I told you, breaking up was my idea. I'm fine."

"Truly?"

I looked down and flipped through the script. "Doesn't call for much scenery, does it? And yes, truly. Where does Cupid come from, by the way? And is there an anti-Cupid in literature, sort of an evil twin who destroys romances?"

She laughed. "Roman mythology. And off the top of my head I can't come up with an opposite, though I'm sure there must be several. Why do you ask?"

"Just wondering."

Observing weekly routine, we reestablished contact with the outer world at five by calling my grandmother (Dad's side) in Florida, then my grandfather (Mom's side) in Arizona. After the calls we ate supper in front of the television. Mom had the local news on. I was still making sketches of Grover's Corners.

"How sad," she murmured.

I glanced at the TV. A bundled-up reporter was facing the camera and at the same time gesturing to some point behind her. "To recap: The county search and rescue team has just called off its day-long search for the missing sixteen-year-old boy believed to have drowned sometime last night in Lake Calhoun. Recovery efforts began this morning after an unidentified jogger discovered the frozen body of a sixteen-year-old girl along the lakeshore. Sources close to the families told LIP that the boy and girl had been dating for about a year and were last seen last night leaving a party where they'd told friends of plans to take the boy's uncle's new ATV out on the lake. The sheriff's department reminds the public that—"

"Hanna—what's wrong?" Mom's voice jolted me back from the dark park and shut off the sound of the four-wheeler's roar. I faced her. She caught her breath when she saw my expression. "Do you think you know them?"

Without understanding how or why I did it, I made a

decision. "No," I said calmly. "I don't know anyone with an ATV. It's just an awful thing, that's all."

Mom glanced back at the TV. "Especially to think of the girl dying that way."

"What way?" I whispered. "I didn't hear it all."

Mom stared at me a moment before answering. "She managed to get out of the lake and to shore before she collapsed. They said tracks showed she'd crawled almost the whole way. She froze to death—can you imagine? I wonder who they are." She clenched her hands together. "Were. Oh god, I hope not any of my kids."

I blocked out the image of the girl crawling across the ice. Blocked out the thought that maybe she believed she was crawling toward help—to a girl on a bench who would get her to safety.

I called Kelsey. "Have you heard the news about those kids dying last night?"

She had and she already knew names. "Lindsey Albright and Derek—"

Derek. I felt my lungs take a punch. Mom moved to my side and squeezed my shoulder.

"—Johnston. She was homeschooled; he went to Brethren."

"Brethren?" I said, looking at Mom and shaking my head. She exhaled and returned to her chair. "How did you find out?" I asked, though it wasn't too hard to imagine. Brethren Academy was a private Christian school several miles away from Humphrey, but in the overall city high school population, there were never many degrees of separation.

Kelsey took a drink of something. "Jessie. Her brother

Scott played on the same club hockey team with the guy, Derek. Maura and Jessie were going to a movie today, but Jessie canceled after Scott got the news from someone on the team. I guess he was all freaked. How are you doing, anyway? Will you be okay over the holiday?"

"What do you mean? It's sad, sure, but I didn't know them."

She sighed. "You broke up with Spence, remember? I'm talking about that."

"Oh, yeah. I'm fine, really. I'd almost forgotten."

Mom pounced as soon as I hung up. "I don't care what you say," she said, "I can tell by your expression that you knew them."

"No," I insisted again. Avoiding her stare, I looked out the window to the snowy world outside. It's worse than that, I thought. I could have kept them from dying.

><

My dreams were not subtle.

Splashing steel-colored water.

A floating figure trapped under ice.

A hand clawing at snow.

A hand clawing at me.

><

"I dreamed about those poor children," Mom said the next morning. "The worst thing of it all is to think about that girl crawling to shore and dying so close to help. How many cars do you suppose passed by? How many people walked past her?"

"Not that many. It was late and cold and who would be out?" I gave her a kiss. "Working 'til three."

All the way downtown I pictured the girl crawling. Where had she gone ashore? Had she remembered me on the bench and sought me? Had she called out? *Girl, girl on the bench, help me.*

If I hadn't been so pissed and left . . . If I had warned them . . .

If.

⇥⇤

The Christmas Eve rush never happened, at least not in swimwear. Still, I expected my manager to ask me to stay and cover for a couple of girls who'd had the nerve to call in sick, but she waved me off at the end of my shift.

The bus home was strangely empty. I swear I hadn't planned to do it, but when it reached my corner, I stayed put and rode all the way to the lake.

The shoreline was crowded with TV trucks, camera crews, and gawkers. Yellow police tape separated official vehicles from the bystanders. There was a cluster of workers on the ice. Right away I regretted giving in to the impulse that brought me here. I walked along the lake path past the mayhem. I passed kids my age who were sobbing, distraught adults, determined reporters.

A pair of wailing girls occupied the bench where I'd sat on Saturday night. A few other visitors were scattered around: a sad older couple holding hands; a tall bearded boy wearing a yellow cap with stripes and a beat-up bomber jacket; an elegant woman chewing her lip and twisting her long red scarf; two young boys praying on their knees in the snow.

At the edge of the frozen lake a small memorial had sprung up. I guessed it marked the spot where the body was found. There were plastic carnations, a white cross, a large framed photo of the couple, a shiny red pinwheel that spun slowly in the light wind, a bundle of flowers wrapped in a cone of purple paper. A reporter stood near the memorial. She pointed her microphone. "Looks like they're bringing in the body," she said to her cameraman. They rushed toward the recovery operation. Most everyone else followed.

I crouched by the memorial. I couldn't look at the picture for very long because their eyes seemed too alive and accusing. There were dozens of notes, crisp from lying in the cold.

We love you, Lindsey.

Peace be with you.

I will miss you both so much.

I reached and separated the stiff folds of paper around the flowers. Pink roses.

Frozen roses.

A biting gust of wind whipped across the lake, whipping up snow and scattering the notes. The florist's cone rocked, then tumbled away in the arms of another wind gust. The paper snagged on the cross and tore open, spilling brittle pink chips over the icy gray snow.

➤❮

After that scene I needed my friends, but no luck there because like most people, they were embroiled either in family Christmas celebrations or family vacations. Not the Martins, family of two. It had been years since Mom and I had gone anywhere over the break, to say nothing of making a big deal out of the holiday.

I'm the only child of two only children. I have no aunts and uncles, no cousins, and two unrelated grandparents who barely even know each other. My dad's dad died years ago. My mom doesn't know her mother, who took off when Mom was only three, choosing to have nothing more to do ever again with husband and daughter. As far as we knew, the woman was still alive, but she was dead to us, just as we assumed we were to her.

A few years ago my grandparents each remarried and acquired a new batch of stepchildren and step-grandchildren. Mom and I were always welcome to join either throng at any holiday gathering. We got along with all those people, but somehow it seemed simpler and more peaceful to stay home. Which was fine, but it meant that I'd be on my own for days before my friends were released from their holiday obligations.

Just as well, really, because I was certain that for at least a few days the accident would be all anyone would be talking about when people got together, and then what would I say?

I saw them that night.

I should have opened my mouth.

I'm alive and they're dead.

I was alive and they were dead.

As soon as I got home, I leaned on the kitchen counter and dropped my head on my arms, calming a sudden spasm of shivers with deep breaths. A moist sweetness filled my nostrils. I looked up and saw the flowers Kelsey had bought for me in their vase on the table.

Pink roses—just like the ones left for Lindsey and Derek at the lake.

Except mine were alive and theirs were frozen.

Thorns stabbed my palm when I yanked the flowers out of the vase and then pierced even deeper as I shoved the bouquet into the trash. I fell back into a chair and looked at the reddening pinpricks on my hand. "I'm sorry," I murmured. "Lin—"

The dead girl's name thickened and clotted on my tongue, refusing to be spoken aloud in the safe, warm kitchen.

When exactly had it happened? The very moment I'd turned my back? As I climbed the stairs to the street? If my head hadn't been buried in my parka and in my bad mood, would I have noticed that the ATV's engine was suddenly silenced or maybe even heard Lindsey's cries for help?

She must have cried out. Engulfed in the sheer terror of the sudden nightmare, with her boyfriend lost in dark water and her own body crushed by pain from the cold and wet—she must have screamed. And no one came to help.

One moment you're flying over snow with the person you love and the next you're plunging into cold dark water toward the end of everything. Just like that.

⇥⇤

Mom and I slept late on Christmas morning. As soon as we made coffee and said hello, we opened our presents. It's one of our rules for all holidays and events involving gifts: Never wait.

Weeks ago we'd decided it was a necklace Christmas. I'd bought her a great jade and silver one and she'd found a gorgeous lapis lazuli for me. Both necklaces looked good with our pajamas. We called my grandparents and Mom checked in with Charles. After shouting hello to him, I left the room so she could give him encouragement about getting through a day that would be crowded with ex-wives and two sets of children.

Family obligations fulfilled, we made a huge breakfast: eggs Benedict, caramel rolls, fruit salad, champagne. She can burn off calories just thinking about dance steps; I'm a soft size eleven.

The Uptown was showing the newest Coen brothers' film, so for once there was no argument about what to see. We walked to the theater and had a good time talking to people as we all waited in the foyer for the ticket counter to open. Pretty soon Mom discovered someone in the crowd who used to be married to a dancer she'd worked with in New York. That was long before me, so I tuned out the merry "Whatever happened to . . . ?" conversation and picked up a flyer for upcoming movies.

"Hanna?" Mom's voice brought me back to earth. "Line's moving, darling."

I focused my eyes to meet her worried blues. She glanced at the flyer as she took it from me. The ad for the next film caught her eye as it had mine. "Oh, honey," she whispered. I turned stiffly and took two steps toward the ticket counter.

"Psychological thriller . . . redefines terror and nightmare . . . unleashes your worst fears."

The Body in the Water.

>‹

My worst fears? 1. Mom dying. 2. The world blowing up. 3. Something happening to Kelsey or Maura. 4. Cancer or some other bad medical thing. 5. Not being able to draw anything ever again.

I threw my sketch pad down on the snow. "Piece of shit."

Mom shifted on her side of the bench. She closed the

book she'd been reading and laid it on her lap. Without looking I knew she'd raised an eyebrow. We hardly ever swore around each other. I suspected she hardly swore around anyone.

"This was a bad idea, Mom."

"I needed to walk after that meal and the movie."

"We aren't walking."

"So we aren't. Are you going to leave that on the snow?" Her teacher's voice. I picked up the pad.

At least we weren't sitting on the very same bench where I'd sat that night. Like a psychic, she'd made a bee-line for it when we'd first reached Calhoun. I'd only managed to redirect her by claiming there was something I wanted to draw in a different spot. There wasn't, of course, which was probably why nothing I'd been drawing was any good.

"All this gray today," she said. "I hate these short winter days. So dark, so early. The color of those plastic flowers is terribly startling, don't you think? And isn't it interesting how those memorials spring up?"

I slammed a hand down on the pad. It only made a soft feeble *thunk*, not a sharp articulate *slap*, because I'd put mittens back on. "Mom, would you just quit dancing around it? If you want to talk, talk." Of course she wanted to. I had no doubt it was the reason that she'd suggested the walk. I'd figured I couldn't turn her down, it was Christmas after all, so when she'd made the suggestion I had insisted we stop by the house so I could get my backpack and supplies to have along as my defense. She always granted me quiet when I was drawing.

Once again, those worried blues. "Do you want to talk, Hanna?"

I scribbled dark lines with the pencil. Its point snagged and ripped a snow-softened spot on the paper. "I thought the movie was too long. Funny, but long."

She sighed. "Their families must be having a terrible day."

Here we go. I flipped to a dry page. More dark lines.

"You're certain that you didn't know either of them?"

"You have already asked that. The answer remains no."

"It's just that—"

"I'm acting too upset? Taking it too hard?"

"Maybe breaking up with Spencer was tougher—"

"Mom, no! Trust me: The only time I even think about Spencer now is when someone feels they have to mention him." She obviously wasn't satisfied. "Okay, maybe those kids dying has bothered me a little." I waved an arm. "This is practically my backyard. They were about my age. And it's a horrible way to die. So sudden, you know? One minute you're having fun and then in an instant you're facing death, just like—"

Our eyes met, then she glanced away. Her jaw tightened and she held very still.

"Just like that," I whispered. I don't think she heard me. I'm pretty sure she was flashing back to a country club dance and her own nightmare Saturday night.

I hugged my drawing pad, cleared my throat, and said, "I didn't know them."

She stuffed her hands into her pockets and seemed to melt into her brown wool coat. She tipped her head. "I bet he did. Poor boy."

The tall boy with the bomber jacket and striped yellow cap I'd seen the day before was walking toward the memorial. He stopped a few feet away from it and stood looking down, one hand stroking his patchy beard, the other slipped into a back pocket. Suddenly he dropped to his knees in the snow. His head fell back and he looked up at something. Tree branches? Birds? Some memory of or wish for a god?

I flipped to a fresh page. I dug in my backpack for the tin of colored pencils.

Streetlamps were flickering on when Mom finally touched my arm and said, "I hate to stop you, but I'm freezing, Hanna. It's gotten so cold. Let's go home."

The park was nearly empty. The boy with the yellow cap was still there, though he'd moved to a bench—my bench. He stared straight ahead, not seeming to breathe or move a muscle, not even when my mother gently touched his shoulder as we passed behind him, our heads bent down against the rising north wind.

→←

Derek and Lindsey were buried together the day after New Year's. The TV stations covered it like a war.

I watched, stunned. Sharing a grave?

I turned to Mom, who had finished eating supper and was now knitting while she watched the news. "If Spence and I had died some way together, would you have done that?"

She finished a row before looking up. "I don't know. Perhaps, though it seems a bit dramatic."

"But just suppose they—we—had been on the verge of a breakup or a fight and no one knew."

She set down the needles and yarn. "I'm not sure that

matters, not if the decision gave me some comfort Why does it bother you so much?"

I had no answer I wanted to give. I pointed to the TV as a reporter corralled some funeral-goers. "Another thing I don't get is why people agree to talk on camera."

The woman being interviewed was so eager to speak, she was practically eating the microphone. Her tears flowed and her words came in gasps: ". . . good Christian kids . . . Sunday school helpers . . . super role models . . ."

I thought of the condom Lindsey had tossed at me. Role-modeling safe sex—is that what the lady meant?

The reporter cornered some friends of the couple. One boy bobbed his head while the girl at his side said, "They had a perfect relationship."

I closed my eyes and pictured Lindsey pounding the moron's shoulder and shouting, "Don't drive like an ass-hole."

I said, "People just don't know."

"Don't know what?" Mom replied in the low monotone she uses when she's not entirely there.

"Other people's hearts. Minds too." I glanced at her. Damn, now I had her full attention.

"Hanna—"

I shushed her and pointed at the television again. "Sorry, I want to watch this." I could feel her studying me, but I resisted the urge to turn and face her. Finally she rose, collected our dishes, and went to the kitchen.

The crowd on television was thinning. I looked for the boy with the striped cap but didn't spot him. No doubt his mother had done him a favor and made him shave and dress up.

I dug my phone out of my coat pocket and called Kelsey. "Did you see the funeral report?" I said.

"I'm watching one now. It's so sad. It could be any of us. We've all gone out on the lakes in winter."

"Sure, but on foot or skis, not in a stupid ATV. I can't believe they buried them together. That's a bit melodramatic."

"You can be such a hard-ass, Hanna."

"I didn't call so you could call me names, okay? Have you ever seen a guy around who wears a bomber jacket and a yellow stocking cap with stripes? He has a bad beard."

"No. Want me to check around?"

Did I? And if we found out who he was, what then? Call him up, introduce myself, and say what?

Gosh, sorry about your friends. I'm the person who spoke with them last.

Ya know, I could have saved them from dying. Wanna get coffee?

"No thanks, Kels. Just wondering."

>←

An hour later I was working in my room on *Our Town* sketches when I heard car doors slam in the driveway. Seconds later a snowball hit my window. By the time I looked out, Maura and Kelsey were already inside the house and noisily greeting Mom. I frantically picked up the drawings I'd been working on earlier, but soon realized that there was no way I could collect and hide them all before the girls burst in. I opened the bedroom door and shouted, "Just a sec. I'll be down."

"Just a sec?" Maura echoed. "What exactly are you doing up there?"

"We've seen your room when it's a pit," Kelsey said.

"And we've seen you naked," Maura added.

"I'll be down," I repeated. I gathered every recent drawing but the *Our Town* work and shoved it all under the bed.

They were in the kitchen with Mom when I finally joined them. They both greeted me with matching puzzled looks. All similarity ended there.

Kelsey normally has a smiling demeanor of complete contentment, which is as false a façade as I've ever seen because the girl's the most competitive person I know, captain of both the math bowl and girls' hockey teams.

Maura almost always has an internal jitterbug going on. Tonight it was in overdrive. She practically bounced in her seat as she stabbed a fork at the contents of a carry-out carton. "What are you hiding in your room?" she said. A rice noodle hung from her mouth. She sucked it in.

"Nothing. I wanted to finish something I was working on. What's that about?"

"My dinner. Very spicy pad Thai. I just got off work. I haven't eaten all day. Weird, how you can work at a restaurant and not eat."

I sat at the table across from her, shaking my head. "Not what I meant. What are those?"

"Yearbooks," my mother answered, flipping through one. "From Southwest, South, and Brethren. I remember this boy." Her finger tapped a shot of some guys playing basketball. "Kelsey, didn't you have a little thing with him once?"

"Kelsey's had dozens of little things," I said. "You'll have to be more specific."

Maura laughed, then swallowed it when Kelsey shot her a look as she took the book from Mom. "Oh, no—Brett Simon," Kelsey said. "That was in eighth grade, Claudia. Eighth grade does not count."

"Lasted longer than that, as I recall," Mom said, rising from the table and squeezing Kelsey's shoulder.

"Ninth grade also doesn't count. I can't believe you remember."

Maura pulled the book over and studied the picture. "I don't remember Brett looking like that. You might want to get reacquainted, Kels."

Mom carried her tea mug to the sink and emptied it. "Did you bring these because you're looking for someone in particular, or are you just checking out old friends?"

Maura and Kelsey waited for me to answer.

"I don't believe this," I said to them. "I make a casual comment about some guy and not even two hours later you've rustled up yearbooks and come storming the house."

"You asked," Kelsey said. "This seemed like a good idea." She riffled pages on one of the books.

"Just trying to cheer up a friend," Maura said. "Kels doesn't entirely agree with me, but I think that maybe you're in a little denial about Spence, and a new guy could be the thing."

"I am not in denial." I looked at Mom. "Enjoying this?"

She nodded. "I am, but maybe it's time I make a discreet exit."

Maura shook her head. "You two are always so bloody polite to each other. It's like you've just met. Blows me away sometimes. My mom—"

Before Maura could dive into the familiar lament about her relationship with her mother, Kelsey gasped. "Oh my god, it's them, those kids who died. This is so strange: They were buried today and I opened it right to their picture."

It was the same picture someone had planted at the memorial: Derek and Lindsey at a Valentine's Day dance. "I saw them . . ." I whispered before I caught myself. Mom slid into the seat next to mine.

"You saw them?" Kelsey asked. "When?"

I felt the heat from the watchful eyes of the three people who knew me best. What would they think about me once they knew I'd let two people drive straight to death just because I was pissed off? "I saw them bring in his body."

"Oh, Hanna," Mom said, "why didn't you say so?"

"Did you see what the body looked like?" Maura asked. Kelsey batted her arm.

I shook my head. "No one could get that close." I turned to Mom. "I didn't want to admit I went and joined the gawkers. You should have seen all the people there. It was sick. I wish I hadn't gone." I turned away from her worried stare and closed the yearbook. I couldn't bear to see the smiling couple. "I asked Kelsey about the boy with the yellow hat we saw at Calhoun on Christmas Day. That wasn't the first time I'd seen him there. He was at the lake when they brought in the body."

"He was so sad," Mom said.

I faced Maura and Kelsey. Their worried expressions matched Mom's. "He was probably one of their friends. I was curious and that's the only reason I asked about him."

Kelsey pushed the *Brethren Record* toward me. "Start looking."

I pushed it back. "It was just a whim."

>+<

After they left, I went to my room before Mom could launch a fact-finding conversation. I hauled out the pictures from under my bed and spread them out across the room. I picked up one of the boy in the yellow hat.

No. Still not right.

I stayed up late drawing. The BoDeans and Rusted Root rotated on the CD player. About three I scanned a few drawings and uploaded them onto my website. I read the stats and smiled. Almost eight hundred people had been there since I checked in last. Eight hundred faceless hits. How had that many people found their way there? I'd told no one that I had the site, there was no name on it, and no way to connect it to me. Of course, I'd embedded a few key phrases and words to snare the search engines: Outsider art. City of Lakes. Twin Cities dining. Vincent van Gogh. Super Bowl highlights. Naughty girls.

I added a few more: ATV accident, Minneapolis memorial, Calhoun drowning.

Six hours later, nine a.m. I didn't hear the knocking and didn't hear the door squeaking, but I sure as hell heard the fear and tension in my mother's voice. "Oh my god, Hanna."

She never entered without my permission. Never. It was one of those unbroken rules that made it possible for us to live side by side. Why change things today? "Get out," I said.

She said, "I knocked hard, but you didn't answer. I

need your *Our Town* sketches, remember? You didn't leave them on the table. I'm having lunch with Tom to go over the construction plans. What is all this?"

I propped myself on an elbow as she did a slow 360 and surveyed the carpet of drawings. The circle completed, she picked up one paper and sat on my bed. I dropped down and covered my head with a pillow.

"You need to see someone, darling. Today. I'll call Ray and get you in. He'll make time."

I made a noise into the pillow. Ray Nixon was an old colleague of my dad's at the U. They'd done their psych residencies together and had shared a practice until Dad died. "Why?"

"Why?" she echoed. She removed the pillow, made eye contact, and gestured broadly. "Because of this."

"I always have a mess of work."

"But this?"

She had me there.

A room full of drawings, but only three subjects: the boy at the memorial site; a body trapped under ice; a fetal-shaped figure on snow.

I said, "I'm fine." I reclaimed the pillow and covered my head. "Go away."

➤‹

The university's department of adolescent and children's psychiatry had been remodeled since I'd last visited, shortly after Dad died. Mom walked in with me, stayed around until I was called, then left for her lunch date with Tom, the freelance set designer and builder Whipple always hired for its shows. I followed the receptionist into Ray's office. He immediately hugged me.

"No chitchat," I said, pulling away and dropping into a chair. "Let's get this over. I know you squeezed me in and you have a real patient coming in soon."

"I can't even get a college update?"

"Ray," I sighed, "it's still Rhode Island. That's the deal with early decision. If they accept you, you're bound to them. Nothing's changed since I saw you three weeks ago at the party Mom gave for Charles's birthday." My breath snagged. Only three weeks ago things were normal?

"Ah," he said with satisfaction. He sat and picked up a legal pad and a pen. "Three weeks. So we have a before and after thing going on. Why?"

Should I try some misdirection? He was a pro, but it might work. "First, I broke up with my boyfriend—" I held up a hand. "Don't get excited. It was time to do it and it's not part of the story. I'm only mentioning it because I know what a crime it is to withhold information during a session."

"What's the real story then?" Staredown. I gave in first and glanced away.

"Those kids who died on the lake?" I said as I looked out his window. "I didn't know them, but I've been drawing the scene over and over. Mom got freaked when she saw the pictures. I guess it's fair to say I've been obsessing." I faced him with a smile.

He tapped the pad and studied me. Those patient eyes, so like my dad's. "Why?" he said softly.

Why not tell him everything? He'd have the flow of self-pity corked in no time. I'd welcome that, but what could he do about the guilt?

Why didn't you warn them, Hanna?

Because I was pissed.

Why were you pissed?

Because they were happy.

There it was: Because they were happy and I wasn't, they were dead. Of course, they hadn't been so happy, not there at the end. Another secret I was sitting on: Their last night on earth hadn't been going so well. The truth—

He leaned forward. "What about the truth, Hanna? You were mumbling something."

"The truth," I said slowly, avoiding his eyes, "is that the whole thing has made me think about Dad. He and I used to spend time on the lake in winter, skiing and skating."

I watched him decide whether to accept this. Since he was obviously having difficulty doing that, I fed him some more. "I often get obsessive with my drawings and I work on the same thing over and over. She overreacted. I think she lived with a psychiatrist for too long and she analyzes things too much and because of the breakup she was especially worried."

His unflinching stare made me nervous and chatty. "I miss my dad, Ray. Having Charles around is great, don't get me wrong, I like him, but it's sort of stirred up memories. Then those kids died in that awful way, and it's Christmas, and I guess you could say I put everything I'm thinking about into my drawings and they turned out dark and I guess that freaked her and that's why I'm here. Please feel free to call her and say I'm fine. I certainly don't feel screwed up."

His pencil tapped against his yellow pad three times. He waited.

Be silent and be patient—two shrink tricks to make

you talk. Well, it wasn't going to work this time. He was not going to win.

Tap. Tap. Tap.

"Ray," I blurted, "why is it that happiness can disappear in an instant but sadness stays around forever?"

His shoulders sagged as he exhaled. "I don't know, Hanna."

"Hell of an answer, Dr. Nixon. I think our time is up, don't you?" I rose and picked up my parka from the chair. "I guess maybe it's because that's just the whole scheme."

"Scheme?"

Another shrink trick: Be a parrot. "Life is short, death is forever. What do you suppose it was like for Mom that night? One minute she's spinning around the club dance floor and then"—I snapped my fingers—"he's gone.

"Just like that," I said after a long silence. "You and Julia were there with them that night. What was it like?"

"It was frightening, Hanna. It was like one of those bad dreams where things just evaporate in your hands and all around you and you can't make it stop."

"I've never had those dreams," I said. "I really don't want to talk anymore, but don't hold it against me on the sanity checklist, okay?"

He rose and held the coat as I slipped my arms into the sleeves. "Have you asked your mother about that night?"

He's not a tall man, maybe my height or a bit taller. I looked at him evenly as I pulled gloves out of a pocket. "It's all so sad, Ray. And now she's got Charles. I think I'll just let it be. You won't tell her that I brought it up, will you? Patient confidentiality and all that."

"Of course not."

"What will you tell her?"

"Hanna, I want to see you again in a week for a full session. Two weeks at the latest. If you'd be more comfortable with a doctor who's not a family friend, I'd understand, and I'd happily refer you to the right person. Either way, I strongly recommend you come back. You're eighteen of course, and it's your decision."

"If I don't?"

"I'll tell your mother you refused. It's my guess she will . . . hover."

I closed my eyes. Already I could feel the weight of her on my back. I said, "Fine."

>‹

The U had already resumed classes after winter break and the campus sidewalks were crowded, but it was early in the day and only a few people waited at my bus stop. I easily scored a window seat when I got on the 16A. I dropped my head against the window, hoping the cold glass would soothe the searing after-burn from the session with Ray. Life, death, happiness, sadness, obsessive art, Spencer, Dad's spectacular exit, and the mother-daughter pact of silence on the subject of his death. Gosh, what had I missed? I moaned, and the lady in the seat ahead of me turned and stared. I crossed my arms in a tight hug and looked away.

A clump of people waited to cross Washington Avenue in front of the bus. The tallest one in the group wore a yellow cap with green stripes. The light changed and everyone moved. He jogged. A U bookstore bag swung heavily from his hand.

A U student? Not impossible, but I wouldn't have

guessed he was that old, especially if he was close to the dead couple, who were both sixteen, according to the news reports. More likely he was post-secondary, doing part or all of his junior- or senior-year classes at the U and getting credit for both high school and college. I'd considered it myself, but hadn't wanted to hassle with commuting between schools every day.

Watching Yellow Cap, I got out of my seat and slid into one across the aisle. He waited in the bus shelter across the street. Well, well—the mystery deepens. No bus he'd catch over there would take him anywhere near the neighborhoods around Lake Calhoun.

The airbrakes wheezed and the bus rocked. The door opened and closed for one more passenger, who landed beside me. "Whew, just made it," she said.

Not wanting to be entirely uncivil but also not wanting to even slightly encourage a conversation, I responded by turning to share a wan smile. When I looked back out the window, Yellow Cap was staring straight at me. We locked eyes until the bus pulled away.

3
Will

"For ten minutes pretend you're my granddaughter. Great-granddaughter, maybe; I just turned eighty."

"Ma'am, I'd be happy to step back in the dressing room when you have the suit on."

"Don't be silly. As busy as the store is, some other customer will have a question and off you'll go. Turn around if you're shy about this."

Too late. Before I could move she'd unhooked her bra and two eighty-year-old breasts were swinging free. I quickly looked down at the stack draped over my arm. "Which suit first?"

"Green one, please."

As I fumbled with the clips on the hanger, I saw her pants drop to her ankles. I kept my eyes aimed at the floor, which was the only safe place to look because the changing-room walls were lined with mirrors.

"Thank you, dear," she said when I handed her the swimsuit. "Those hanger clips are so hard for me to deal with. My arthritis." She made a few ugly noises as she wiggled into the suit. "What do you think?"

I looked. "Great fit. You're in really good shape."

My pretend-grandmother struck a pose. "Yoga and swimming, thank you very much." She turned her back to me. "Does it cover my ass?"

"Yes, ma'am, it certainly does."

She touched her toes. "Still covered?"

"Yes, ma'am." I glanced up at the smoky glass ceiling and made a face for the surveillance cameras.

Thirty minutes later she walked away from the register—the happy, Florida-bound owner of six new ass-covering swimsuits. "No more customers for me until after I've had my break," I said to one of the other clerks. "I'll be working in the back."

The store had been busy all day and the dressing rooms were trashed with rejected suits. I walked into each vacated room, scooped up the merchandise, and hauled it down to the recovery table at the far end of the changing area. I dumped the load and began rehanging.

I'd worked my way through half of the pile when my boss tapped my shoulder, startling me out of a Rufus Wainwright reverie. "Whoa, Diana," I said. "Scared me." She was frowning. "Was I humming too loud?"

She tipped her head. "A boy is asking for you, but he doesn't know your name."

My hands froze above a pink and white one-piece. "Then how could he ask for me?"

"He described you. He seems a little . . ." She made a face and shrugged her shoulders. "Scruffy, maybe. A bit rude. Not at all like that sweet Spencer."

I looked at the dressing room exit. "How did he know I was here?" I murmured.

Diana touched my arm. "Should I call security?"

"No. I'll go."

The minute I walked out, he dropped his eyes and studied the floor. Not rude, I thought as I walked toward him, just shy.

The other clerks were lined up and watching. No doubt Diana or one of the others had a hand on the phone and was ready to call security.

"Where's the hat?" I said. "I've only ever seen you with that yellow cap."

He smiled slightly and patted his pocket.

I turned around and made a sign to the clerks: *It's okay.*

"Do you get a break?" he said, looking shyly at the floor again, which was fine with me, as it gave me time to check him out. A little over six feet tall, chin-length auburn hair that was hat-smashed on top and wavy at the bottom, broad shoulders under the unzipped jacket. There was the half-assed beard, of course, behind which peeked patches of soft perfect skin. A plain navy T-shirt with a slightly frayed collar. Old jeans, with shrapnel-like holes around one knee. Scuffed brown Doc Martens.

"I get a dinner break at five. Why?"

He raised his eyes. Large and dark blue. Holy crap. Trouble ahead, Hanna.

"I've seen you around," he said.

"The U, last Monday."

He nodded. "First day of classes. Do you go there?"

I shook my head. "I'm a senior at Humphrey. And I've seen you at . . . the lake."

"The lake, yeah." He reached out and tapped my name

tag. "Hanna." He repeated it, whispering the second time. He pulled his hand back and stuffed it into a pocket. "I think that maybe we should talk."

>‹

He looked up from his soup bowl as I dropped into a chair. "I didn't wait. Sorry. I've hardly eaten all day."

"Don't apologize. It's not as if this is a date or anything. I don't even know your name. Who are you?"

"Will Walker. Hanna what?"

"I don't know if I want to tell you that yet. I don't know who you are, Will Walker. How did you even know where I worked?"

He put down his spoon and sipped some Coke. He studied the glass, then sipped again. That sad beard. How soft was it?

I got busy with my dinner. I peppered my pasta salad, spread a napkin, drank some Coke. Anything to stop myself from rubbing a finger against his chin.

"Yesterday I was waiting on Nicollet to transfer buses," Will said. "I saw you get off your bus and go into the store. I followed you, Hanna."

I sat back. My hands dropped onto the table. The desire to touch him was no longer a problem. "You did *what?*"

"I lost you when I got behind this lady and a stroller on the escalator and you ran on up. I cruised around the store for a while and then I spotted you working."

"Do you have any idea how incredibly creepy that is?"

He nodded. "My sisters said you'd feel that way and that I probably shouldn't tell you." He leaned forward. "Well, Hanna No Last Name, do you have any idea how incredibly creepy it is to discover a drawing of yourself on someone's anonymous website? And don't tell me you didn't do it, because I know you did. I saw you sketching on Christmas Day at Calhoun. Was that your mother you were with?"

I nodded and poked at my salad.

"Well, my mother is an art historian and she's worked for years at the art institute. She knows her stuff and she loved the one you did of me. She said I stand like that all the time. She especially liked how you had the red sprayed all over. I said it was blood—more creepiness, if you ask me—but she thought you meant it as a light, maybe coming from the pinwheel."

"Your mother saw the website?" I closed my eyes. Had I taken down *Dogs in Heat*? I drummed on the table. Yes, pretty sure.

"The whole family, if you must know. One of my sisters was surfing and she came across it—"

"How did she get there?"

"I don't know exactly, but she was searching for stuff about the accident. She spends hours online. She's a . . . writer for an ad agency and she's always looking for unusual things. She recognized me in one of the drawings and had us all take a look. As I said, it was incredibly creepy."

I said, "My name is Hanna Martin."

He offered his hand across the table. I'm not sure, but I think I may have dragged my index finger across the back of his hand as we let go after shaking. Entirely accidental.

Will said, "They were friends of yours?"

I sat back. Puzzled. "No. But you knew them, right?"

He ran fingers through his hair as he appraised me. He

shook his head. "I didn't know them. So all those draw-ings—it was just because you found it interesting subject matter? Because you were curious? People you don't even know die like that and you just go ahead and draw it?"

"No . . ." I started, then lost the words under the heat of accusing dark blue eyes.

His frown deepened. "Didn't it occur to you that maybe their parents or friends might see the drawings? Can you imagine how they'd feel, Hanna? My mom got freaked enough and she didn't even know them."

"Will. Please, I—" I clenched my hands, holding back. Holding everything back.

"Sorry," he said. "The whole thing's just kind of . . . sad."

Sooner or later it was bound to spill out. Sooner or later I'd have to tell someone or else sooner or later I'd burst. Why not unload it all now? Will didn't know Derek and Lindsey and so how could he hate me for let-ting them die? Even better, he didn't know me, so any judgment he dished out couldn't possibly matter.

"I'm not a voyeur, Will. That's not why I drew all those pictures. I talked to them right before they died. I was down by the lake because I'd just dumped my boyfriend and I wanted to think about it and they came by and stopped to be obnoxious the way happy people can be and I got pissed because I wanted to be alone and so I didn't tell them about the thin ice that some skiers had just warned me about. And then I left. And then they died."

He blinked. Slumped.

"No one knows, Will. I haven't told anyone else I talked to them. I haven't told anyone else that I could have prevented it. And I could have, except for my bad mood. My mood, Will—that's why they're dead. My *mood*. I was in a lousy mood and, oh god, I wish it was all different."

He broke apart a slice of bread. He stared at the pieces, then set them both down on his plate. "Hanna, it's not like you could have stopped it from happening."

"I think I could have. I could have said something and then maybe they'd be alive."

"Maybe."

" 'Maybe' is awful enough." I'm not sure he heard me. He'd slipped inside himself somewhere. I watched, wondering what sort of struggle was going on. "I don't think I could have told you all that if they were your friends. Please don't tell anyone." He nodded. I hoped it was a promise. "That's why I drew those pictures and why I went to the lake those times I saw you. I can't stop thinking about that night."

He nodded again, but still didn't look up.

"What about you? If you didn't know them, why were you there?"

At last Will looked up. His eyes focused on me. He said, "I'm the one who found her body."

⊰⊱

I wasn't the only one who'd been holding back a story. His poured out.

He always jogged early in the morning, he explained. He played baseball, and he ran at least seven miles a day all through winter to keep in shape for the season. Normally he ran along the Mississippi River, which was close to his house, but he'd spent the night at his grandparents' and so that morning he ran around the lakes instead.

It was so cold that no one else was running, not at six
a.m.

It was still more dark than light at that time of day.
What light there was played tricks on the eye.

That looked like a body.

Couldn't be.

Go back.

Couldn't be.

Some distance later he stopped, jogged in place,
turned, and ran back. He walked the final few yards, slowing down with each step as he approached the silver
mound on the snow. He leaned over, looking. Kneeled
down, reaching. Fell back, gasping. The depths of his
lungs filled with sharp frigid air as he dug into a pocket
for the cell phone, the cries for help already rising in his
throat.

A torn candy wrapper flapped against the toe of a
frozen shoe.

A gust of wind cleared drifted snow, revealing a stiff
curled hand.

Dark eyes stared blankly from behind a thick cocoon
of ice.

>‹

"Your drawings of the body weren't right."

Still speechless from his story, I could only shrug. The
busboy came by and asked for our dirty dishes. We both
signaled that he could take them away.

"I should get back to work," I said when the table was
clear.

"She wasn't curled up like you had her in the drawings."

"Will, please. Maybe the whole thing is something we
should be forgetting."

He stretched out his arms. "It was like she was lunging for something or had jumped and crashed. She was coated in ice, even her face was covered. That's how I knew she was dead." He swore softly. "One minute I'm running along and thinking about the cinnamon rolls my grandpa was putting in the oven when I left the house and then the next thing I'm doing is looking at a dead girl."

"There was nothing about you on the news, just that an unidentified jogger had found the body."

He shrugged. "I'm a minor." His eyes met mine for the first time since he'd described her body. "If you're not eighteen, they can't . . . Oh, Hanna, it's sort of complicated."

I picked up my purse and rose from the table. "I'm off work at eight. Can you hang around?" He nodded. I hugged him. "Meet me in the bookstore across the street."

>‹

He was reading a graphic novel in the teen section when I finally escaped swimwear. He'd sunk deep into a big chair—legs spread, jacket unzipped, yellow cap on his head. He was glued to the book. I stood over him. He still didn't notice me. I tapped the cap. He glanced up and raised a finger: *Wait, please.*

It was kind of fun to watch him. His eyes worked their way across and around the page slowly. His lips pressed together and then relaxed in response to something he saw or read. His fingers fanned out across the covers. The right index finger moved slowly up and down.

He finished and looked up at me. "That was kind of annoying, you watching."

"Sorry." Not really; I'd enjoyed it too much.

He reshelved the novel and zipped his jacket. "Let's go there. I want to go there with you."

Friday night. The other people getting on the bus all looked wasted from a long week of work. "Look at everybody," Will said after we'd sat down. "It's like we're in a night of the living dead."

I dropped my head against the window. "I wish I could bring back the dead. I wish myself back all the time."

Will turned in the seat until he was facing me. "Hanna," he whispered sharply, "don't do that. Don't blame yourself anymore."

I cupped his neck with my hand, pulled him closer, and kissed him.

When the person behind us cleared his throat, I gently pushed Will away.

He took my hand. "Wow," he said. "I didn't expect this."

Tell me.

Only after we got off the bus at the lake did it hit me how poorly dressed I was for a walk in the cold. I had my parka and gloves, but I'd worn dress shoes, thin socks, and unlined pants. The wind tore across the lake and chilled me to the bone.

The memorial had been stripped and scattered by the wind. Will collected and neatly repositioned things. I stood behind the shield of a tree, getting colder by the second.

"This is new since I was here last," he said. He held up a fist-sized stuffed bear.

"How can you be sure all that belongs here? You could have just gathered up any old trash that was left in the playground and got blown over."

He fingered a ribbon on the bear and tilted it to catch the light from the streetlamp. "I 'heart' Lindsey," he read.

"Let's go, Will. I'm freezing."

He set the bear down carefully among the other memorial items. "I couldn't touch her. I wish I had, Hanna. Someone should have held her hand or done something before she got zipped up in a bag. Is that too weird? I wanted to wait by her. Protect her. You see, the real story is that even before I called 911 I called my sister and she told me to get out of there fast before the cops came. You didn't hear anything about me on the news because I left. No one but my family and you knows who that unidentified jogger is. I should have stayed with her. I wish I hadn't listened to my sister."

I touched his arm. "Why did she tell you to leave?"

"We didn't know how the girl had died. Beth was certain that if it looked like a murder, the cops would suspect me and hold me for questioning. Even if they didn't think I'd done anything, she said it would get to be a huge thing, especially once the reporters arrived. 'Boy finds dead body'—that's not a headline my family would be wild about. So I ran. I left her."

"Why didn't you call your parents?"

"They were out of town. That's why I was at my grand-parents'. Beth's a lawyer. I knew she'd know what to do. My dad's a lawyer too, but he—" Will bit down on his lip. "When my parents found out, they had a big fight, worst I've ever seen. They didn't even try to hide it from us. Mom thought it was the right thing to do. Dad didn't. I should shut up."

I grabbed his hand and tugged. "Let's get hot chocolate."

⇥⇤

The coffee shop was crowded and bright. Will put his hands on my shoulder and pointed me toward the only open table. "Go grab it. I'll get the drinks. My treat; I'm loaded with Christmas money."

I was still deep-chilled from the walk and his confession. As I waited for Will at the table—my head spinning with the things I wanted to know about him—I kept my parka on and even left the hood up. When I finally pushed it back, a woman was standing over me, staring.

"Oh my goodness," she said. "You're here, you're alive."

I'd only ever seen her face in the dark, but I knew the voice. Skier Two. I peered closely. Late twenties, I guessed. Single long brown braid hanging down the front of her shoulder. Wire-frame glasses and beautiful brilliant red lipstick.

She collapsed into the chair I'd been saving for Will. "Marie and I were so sure it was you. We thought you were the girl who froze."

I said, "Please go. I'm waiting for someone."

No such luck. "We decided you'd had a fight with your boyfriend and that's why you were at the lake. You were in such a mood."

I shifted in my seat. Where was Will?

"We figured he came by to get you and then the two of you made up and went for a ride. I was so sure it was you."

My head moved slowly from side to side. "I was the girl you talked to that night. The rest of your story is obviously wrong."

"I'm so relieved."

Will appeared with the drinks. "I got them to go. There's a folksinger starting in five minutes and I don't think I want to hang around for that."

Skier Two looked up. "Is this your brother?"

"Friend."

"You could be brother and sister; you're both tall and dark-haired."

Will said, "I'll find another chair."

She grabbed his arm. "I'm leaving." She shook her head and swore. "Now I'm actually glad we broke up. I always gave in to her."

"You broke up because of me?" I practically shouted.

"Of course not, but that night sure stirred things up. And if I hadn't been so concerned with keeping Marie happy, we might have stayed there with you and run into that couple and warned them. Their ATV went into the lake right at that spot, did you know? They showed the tracks on the news reports."

As Skier Two stood, she figured it out. She leaned on the table toward me. "Did you see them?" she asked. "Did you try warning them? They must have been there right after we left. The newspaper article—"

"No one could have prevented it," Will said. "Warning them would have done nothing at all. They were two idiot teenagers having fun and no one can stop that train."

Skier Two eyed him. "I suppose. Still"—she turned back to me—"did you see them?"

Again, Will to the rescue. "Would you please get off the subject?" He didn't do harsh well, but it caught her attention. "I'm the person who found the girl's body that next morning, okay? I don't much like reliving the scene. Hanna knows that, but she didn't want to say anything. Now you know, so would you leave us alone?"

What else could she do? She put a hand on his shoulder as she turned to leave. "You poor boy."

"You didn't have to tell her, Will," I said when she was gone. "But thanks; it worked."

"Hardly matters now, I guess. Besides, she doesn't know my name."

The hot chocolate wasn't cool enough to drink. We just sat there—knees touching under the table—cradling our cardboard cups and not speaking until the folksinger appeared at the front of the room. Under cover of the weak applause, I said, "Let's go."

><

Our drinks had reached a perfect temperature by the time we hurried the four blocks to my house. I dropped my coat onto a living room chair and took a sip. "Want some cookies to go with this?"

He nodded as he looked around. "This house is a lot newer than the others in the neighborhood."

"The one that used to be here burned down. My parents bought the lot and built this right before I was born. It's the only place I've ever lived."

"Me too. I mean my house, of course. It's even the only place my dad's ever called home."

"Was it your grandparents'?"

He shook his head as he stood in front of the piano studying family photos. "No. He just got moved around a lot when he was a kid, so when he and Mom bought the house a couple years after they were married, it meant a lot to him. She's wanted something bigger for ages but he doesn't want to leave." He pointed to a picture. "You and your parents?"

"That's us."

"Where are they tonight?"

"Mom's out with friends. Dad died six years ago."

He followed me into the kitchen. "Your dad's dead? I guess there's lots we don't know about each other."

"Well, that's not surprising, right? What about your parents?"

He took a drink before answering. When he'd swallowed, he looked at the cup before looking at me. "Both home because of the holidays. They've been gone a lot for work."

"Why is your mom gone so much? Seems unusual for art historians to travel."

He shrugged. "I think a lot of them do, actually. She never has before, though, mostly because Dad's always in . . . because Dad has to. But this year she got a fellowship to study at different museums. She's been in Chicago lately. They're both home almost every weekend." He frowned. "They weren't that weekend, though. They were at a wedding in Boston."

"So when they're gone you stay with your grandparents?"

"Sometimes. My sisters are sort of between things and are at the house a lot. Let's skip the family talk. Unless you want to tell me something. I'd like that. You could tell me about your dad. That must be tough, him being gone and all."

"I will tell you about him, but some other time." I set

my cup down and put my arms around him. I couldn't believe I was being so bold. I'd never been that way with Spence.

He blushed. "Okay." His breathing seemed to quicken. "So, what?"

"So . . . do you think your mom would like that drawing of you?"

His eyes widened. "Yeah. She'd love it."

I pulled away. "I've got a couple. You can pick. I'll get them. The cookies are in the cupboard by the fridge."

Halfway up the stairs I realized he'd skipped the cookies and just followed me. I paused, my hand gripping the banister. He bumped into me. "Oops," he said.

My room was reasonably neat. After the thing with Mom, I'd picked up most of the papers and put them out of sight. It's a large room. There's my bed, of course, pushed into the corner with windows. I have a drafting table in the middle of the room and two mismatched dressers. One's for clothing, the other holds my art supplies. There are a couple of chairs, an easel, my stereo, and a computer desk. No posters, just my own paintings and drawings on the walls. Will looked at them all, one after another, taking his time. I pulled the stack of drawings I wanted out of a drawer and sat cross-legged on the bed, waiting for him to finish his survey.

He came to a series of small pastels on the wall near the computer. "These are different than the others," he said. "Something about the color. I like everything, but these are really nice. And I like how you etched out the titles across the bottom." He leaned closer and read aloud. "*Big Island Sunrise. Aging Dude and Surf-*

board. *Dancer at Fifty. Lava Flow. Self-Portrait at Sunset.*"

"I did them on a trip to Hawaii last summer. They're really just silly postcards."

He shook his head. "They're good." When he'd finished his circuit around the room, he sat beside me, took the drawings from my lap, and started going through them.

Concentration, I decided at that moment, can be very sexy.

He came to several of him at the memorial site. "Still creepy?" I asked.

His head moved slightly. "No. You're really gifted, Hanna."

I sighed. "Most of the time when I look at my stuff, all I can think about is how much I don't know and how much I need to learn."

He held up a drawing. "This is the one, right?"

"That's it. Take more, if you'd like."

"One for now. You know what's a really weird thing I want to tell you?"

"I have no idea."

"I shouldn't, because it's so self-absorbed. I mean, you invite me up here—"

I hadn't, of course.

"—and let me look at your work, which in a way is like looking at someone naked—"

It's not, of course.

"—and then the first thought that pops into my head to say is . . ." He took a deep breath. Shook his head.

"Holy crap, Will, just say it."

"As good as you are at drawing and stuff, I'm that good at baseball." He didn't seem to mind that I laughed. He tapped the papers on my head. "I'm going to be the all-city third baseman this year, just wait. I'll blow the conference apart." He sat back against the wall, smiling as I continued to laugh. "I'll play college ball for a year," he said, "even if I get drafted by the pros right out of high school, because Mom would kill me if I ever said a single word about going pro that quick. One year of college, then I'll go pro." I began to laugh again. He leaned over and kissed me.

"How long have I known you?" I said when he pulled back. I reached for the light. "Never mind, I don't really want an answer."

He held my hand. "Wait. Don't."

Fine.

"I've never . . . Have you?"

"I went with a guy for a long time, Will, and yes, we did after a while. Look, I was turning off the light. You were kissing me. I'm not sure that necessarily adds up to Let's do it." Well, then again . . .

He nodded. "Yeah," he said softly, looking at his hands. He clenched them into fists, then let them drop open onto his lap. "I can't believe I told you all that about wanting to touch her. I haven't told anyone that."

"I haven't told anyone else about talking to them."

"It's nice to get it out."

"Yes."

Minutes passed; we didn't talk, we hardly moved, for that matter. His knee rested against my thigh and my hand lay on his knee.

"So, where do you think you'll go to school next year?" I said finally.

That luscious hair half-hid his face as he looked down. He tucked it behind an ear. "I'll have another year at South."

Ah, a junior then. Well, fine. "How do you like doing post-secondary?"

His brow furrowed.

"Remember—I saw you the day you started classes at the U."

"Oh. Yeah. I just take a couple of math classes I can't get at South. Hanna, I'm really torn right now. I can't decide what I want more—to talk and learn everything about you or to let you turn out the light."

"Let's talk. But not just about me. Tell me more about playing baseball. I've never been to a baseball game, not even once." I dropped my head back against the wall and closed my eyes. "Go on, talk," I murmured.

He said, "Uh-uh," and turned out the light.

Moments later he whispered, "Wow, it unhooks in front; I like that."

Moments later I said, "Ah, boxers; I like that."

What can I say. Two idiot teenagers having fun. You can't stop that train.

→←

Who would talk first? He shifted his head and his chin grazed my cheek. The beard wasn't exactly soft, but it wasn't scratchy or rough either. More like one of the natural yarns Mom loved to knit with. Mohair, I thought, rubbing a finger along his chin.

He propped up on an elbow. "Wow," he said. "Now I totally understand why the guys who've done it get so crazy about . . . this."

This.

He reached and switched on the lamp. I turned from the sudden brightness. He moved the lamp around until only the edge of its beam fell on the bed. "I want to see you," he said. He pushed back the covers. I watched his studious eyes follow his hand as it moved from my shoulder down to my hips. "Hanna, you meant it, right, when you said it was okay to go ahead like we did?"

I nodded.

"I mean I absolutely would never have done this without using something except you said it was okay when I asked."

I nodded again.

"Hanna, aren't you going to say anything?"

"Guess I'm still in shock," I whispered.

"No lie. I totally didn't expect this."

"It's not as if *I* planned it. Will, it's all fine. I've been on the pill since last fall. And if it was your first time, and my boyfriend—*ex*-boyfriend—and I had only been with each other, and by the way, he and I only—"

He put his finger on my lips. "I don't need the details." He rolled onto his back. "My sisters would absolutely kill me if they thought I'd, you know, without being careful."

Those sisters. "Well, I'm certainly not going to tell them about 'you know.'"

><

When we pulled into his driveway, one of the sisters was opening a side door of their house as she balanced a pizza box. She turned around as my headlights swept across the snowy yard. I leaned over to give him a kiss, but he quickly opened the car door and got out. "Not so fast," I said.

He turned around slowly, then got back in. Once the

sister was safely in the house, he leaned over and kissed me.

"Which one was that? The lawyer or the writer?"

"The lawyer. Beth."

"She lives with you?"

He shook his head. "Not exactly. She just bought a condo, but it's not ready yet, and she had to get out of her old place. Hanna, let's run away." After I laughed he said, "I'm sort of serious."

"Being sort of serious isn't really good enough for running away, Will. On the other hand, why not? We met tonight, we had sex tonight, why not run away tonight?"

He nodded, still glum, still staring at his house.

"Hell, we could fly to Vegas and get married. Oh— maybe not. You're not eighteen yet, right?"

Again, the slight nod.

"Besides, if we ran away, you'd miss baseball season."

That earned me a withering stare, one I bet he'd practiced for years on the sisters. "I'd just like to enjoy being with you without it getting complicated," he said.

"Too late for that." I turned so I could study him. The porch light from his house barely penetrated the shell of the car, but it was enough to illuminate the sweet serious frown on his face. "Let's go back to my house right now, Will," I said. "My mom won't be home for hours."

The frown morphed into a smile. "Too late for that too because they know I'm here. I'd invite you in, but . . ." He shrugged.

"That's okay. I'm not exactly ready to meet the family."

"Once they meet you, everyone will weigh in and have an opinion."

"An opinion about me, you mean."

"About us. When I tell them that you're the girl who did those pictures . . ." He slumped down in the seat and stared at his house.

"I see what you mean. My mom won't be so thrilled either. She'll analyze things. I can just hear her saying that it's too emotionally complicated."

"Exactly. But you know what's even worse is that once they get used to how we met, they'll just take you over."

"Take me over?"

"My family's close. We don't let a lot of outsiders in, not like we used to, but anyone who gets near us tends to get sucked in pretty good."

"So, fine: Let's run away. Who's that looking out the window?"

"My mom. I just want you for myself, Hanna."

"You are so sweet, Will."

He opened the door. "You're going to hate me tomorrow," he said. "I know it."

"Not if you meet me after work like we planned."

He nodded. "Bookstore at seven."

I drove away and circled the block. Before I reached his house again I pulled over and killed the engine and lights. I locked the doors and sat in the dark. The Seward neighborhood is a mixed area, with blue-collar, student, and emigrant enclaves on the north and west side of the neighborhood and well-off professionals clustered on the east near the Mississippi River. Will's home was in between, a modest house on the corner of a block of similar houses.

The blinds over the living room window were half open. I could occasionally see figures moving around.

Were the sisters grilling him about the evening and teasing him about the long good night in the driveway?

A light went on in a second-floor window. Through the blinds I could see a tall silhouette. It moved back and forth across the room a few times. "Go home, Hanna," I said.

The figure stopped. It peeled a shirt off overhead and dropped it to the floor. Arms fell to hips. Yes, that had to be Will, standing with his hands in his pockets, no doubt. Concentrating on something.

"Go home," I said again. "*This* is creepy."

He stood so still. Was he regretting what had happened? Did I?

I turned and reached behind my seat for the drawing pad I kept in the car. The silhouette was too interesting. I wanted to get it down now because there was no way I could capture that light and shadow from memory.

I crawled over the gear shift into the passenger seat and sat cross-legged. Just as I flipped open the pad, the door to his house opened and two people came out. One ran down the steps and jogged in place as she ate a slice of pizza. One leaned back into the house.

His sisters. The one on the stoop held the door open, and then a third person came out, pausing on the top step to pull on gloves or mittens. His mother.

"Don't come this way," I said. "Please don't come this way."

They reached the sidewalk and turned in my direction. I slid down until my head was almost level with the dash. I didn't want to be seen, of course, but I was dying to see them.

What if they recognized the car? They were getting near and I didn't dare climb back in the driver's seat and leave. If they saw the car start up and move, they'd definitely take a good look. Sure, it was a blue Honda and, yes, there had to be a million of those in Minneapolis, but what if the lawyer or the mother had noticed my plates or noticed the orange Whipple parking permit?

Oh hell, the hula dancer. No way they'd have missed that. I pulled it off the dash. The Velcro fastener ripped loudly.

The taller of the sisters was talking and the other two women were laughing. A horn honked nearby; they turned and looked toward the street as they marched in step toward me.

Holy crap, even if they didn't recognize the car, if they noticed someone sitting alone they'd look twice, and then when I finally did meet them, maybe it would hit them: You were the girl in the car late that night. I slid lower and dropped to the floor, curling up into a ball and wedging myself under the dash. My pants soaked up snow that had dropped off Will's shoes.

How long would it take them to pass me? What if one of them needed to stop and blow her nose or something and they were still there when I popped up? Worse, what if someone came out of a house and they all stood by my car enjoying a midnight chat with a neighbor? How would I know?

I counted to fifty, all the while imagining three faces peering in the car window.

My leg tingled and threatened to fall asleep. "Screw this," I said after I'd reached fifty for the second time. I wiggled loose, uncurled, and sat up on the seat. No faces at the window. I twisted and looked just as the three women crossed the street at the end of the block. They turned a corner and disappeared. I tossed my sketch pad onto the backseat, climbed behind the wheel, started the car, and escaped.

><

Will sat on the floor of the children's section in the bookstore. He had a kid leaning on each arm, and two perched at his knees. I stopped a few feet away and listened. He was pretending to have trouble reading an animal counting book.

"I see four hippos," he said slowly.

"No!" the kids shouted together. "Two cows!"

He turned the page, inhaled deeply, and then blew air out in a long noisy breath. "One elephant."

"No! Three ducks!"

It took a long time to reach ten kittens.

"Did you stage that?" I said when he had finally shaken off the children and we'd left the store. "I bet you did. I bet you had a lookout, and the moment I was spotted you started performing."

"How cynical." He kissed me and then took his hat out of a pocket and pulled it on. "I was looking for a birthday present for a cousin and I was just browsing around and then there were all these kids with me. Darn, I forgot to buy her something."

"Do you want to go back in?"

"No, I'll just add my name to my sisters' gift. What do you want to do?"

"A movie, maybe? My mom's got the car tonight and I can't drive you home, so maybe we should go to a theater in Uptown." I rattled off the titles of the films showing at the theaters there. He wasn't thrilled with the choices. "You suggest something, then."

"I know what I don't want to do," he said. "I don't want to go to the lake. I think I've made my last visit to the spot."

I couldn't say that, but I was relieved he didn't want to make the trek tonight. "I don't either. Last night I nearly froze to death."

We took a moment to let the words disappear in the air.

Will rubbed my arm as a bus approached. "Okay if we go to your place?"

I made a face. "I figured we'd end up there, Will; that's fine. Mom's out again. I want to too, but couldn't we do something else first?"

"Give me a break, Hanna. I'm not an animal."

I tapped his chest. "I see four hippos."

The bus door opened and Will nudged me on. He stood very close behind me as I stopped to dig out my fare card. His arm reached around and he dropped in quarters for both of us.

We fell into seats right behind the driver. "What I was going to suggest," he said, "was let's stop at Lunds for marshmallows and stuff and then go to your place and make Rice Krispie treats. I've been craving them all day."

>←

Will sat up. He reached over to the window and scratched a heart in the frost. I lifted the sheet and he slid back down. I rubbed his chest. "I have a confession."

"Let me guess."

"You can't."

"Can too. I bet when I was in the bathroom you went downstairs and ate the rest of the Rice Krispie treats."

I thumped his stomach. "You mean the two pieces that aren't already in there? Guess again."

"You were kidding about being on the pill."

"I would never joke about that."

"You win. I give up."

"After I left you last night I parked down the street from your house. Is your bedroom upstairs, on the west side of the house?"

He nodded. "Did you watch me undress or something?"

"Not really; the shades were mostly closed. I did see your mother and sisters go out. They walked right by my car, but I don't think they saw me. They couldn't have, actually." I described the way I'd wedged myself under the dash.

He laughed. "I should be creeped out, I suppose, but it's too funny. Lucky you didn't get stuck."

"The three of them looked so happy to be together."

"They didn't want to watch the movie Dad and I had picked out, so they went to a tavern to play darts and have a bedtime beer. Sure they were happy. I bet you and your mom like being together."

"We do, but it's different. There's only the two of us."

He combed his fingers through my hair. "You really miss him, don't you?"

"I do."

"Grandparents?"

"Two. Mom's dad and Dad's mom. They've both

remarried a couple of times, but I don't know the steps very well. I guess I should count them, but I don't."

"I only have two too: Mom's mom and stepdad. I do count him because he's been around forever. Her dad died when she was a kid."

"There's a third, actually. My mom's mom is alive, but she's never been around. She took off when Mom was three."

His hand lightly rubbed my neck. "Wow—my dad's mom took off too. He was about six. His dad was never in the picture, so he grew up in a whole bunch of foster homes after she left. He never really had a family until he married Mom and became part of hers."

"Foster homes? I shouldn't complain."

He kissed the spot he'd been massaging. "You weren't complaining."

"I guess I'm lucky. I guess—" I sat up. "Holy crap, she's home. Get dressed." The garage door rumbled noisily. Will reached for the light. "Don't." I scooped up his clothes and threw them on the bed. "She always hits the opener a couple of houses away, which means she's almost at the driveway now and she'd see the light go on and when she meets us downstairs she'd know. God, she's never home this early on Saturdays."

We made it. Will and I were both downstairs and sitting innocently in the kitchen eating the last two Rice Krispie treats when Mom walked in.

By all accounts my mother is the world's best high school teacher. All the people who have told me that have different explanations for why she's so good, but I know that the real reason she's an ace teacher is that she loves and enjoys teenagers. So the moment she walked in the back door and saw a new high school kid sitting in the kitchen with me, her face lit up. When it did, I could sense Will relax. He rose and did the shy smile thing for her.

She waited for me. When I missed my cue she held out her hand. "Claudia Martin."

He looked at the Rice Krispie treat in his hand. "It's kind of sticky with marshmallow. Sorry. Will Walker."

She started to say something, but then suddenly the smile ratcheted down in intensity. She pulled back her hand.

I'd seen it at the same instant: a small white square poking out of the front of his T-shirt collar. Will had put his shirt on backwards.

I jumped in. "Why are you home so early?"

She studied Will. He studied the Rice Krispie treat. He couldn't have known what we'd seen, but he'd felt the mood change. He wilted back into the chair.

"Charles's daughter went into labor," she said. "He went to the hospital to wait."

"That's great, isn't it? I mean, she's overdue, right? I bet her husband's going nuts about now."

"I'm sure," she murmured. "Have we ever met before, Will?"

"You haven't," I said.

Mom didn't take her eyes off him. "You seem familiar."

Will and I exchanged looks. His pleaded, *Help!*

"Hey, the car's here now, so I can drive you home," I said. "Should we go?"

He nodded and rose.

Mom said, "You don't drive, Will?"

He pasted on a smile, more panicked than shy. "City boy, city buses."

Mom nodded slowly. "Good night, then. Nice to meet you."

She was halfway up the steps when we went to the living room for our coats. He put on his bomber jacket and she stopped in her tracks. "Oh my goodness," Mom said. "I know who you are: that boy at the lake."

"Don't wait up," I said as I pulled him into the kitchen. Fat chance, of course. I heard her resume her slow climb up the steps, heard the floor creak as she walked through the upstairs hall. As I opened the back door I froze. Will had followed me out of the bedroom when we'd rushed out. I hoped he'd closed the door.

>‹

His family must eat a lot of pizza. "Don't you ever have it delivered?" I said as the lawyer sister walked past the car. She pounded the car hood with one hand while she balanced the pizza box with the other. She signaled us toward the house. When we didn't move, she shrugged and went inside. I said, "I need to get home. You should turn your shirt around before you go in."

He zipped his jacket up to the collar. "The pizza place we like doesn't deliver. Don't hate me tomorrow."

"Please stop saying that. I won't. Not tomorrow, not ever."

Someone was watching through the window. We ignored her and shared a long, sweet good-night kiss. When I finally pushed him away and started the engine, he opened the car door. Cold air rolled in. "Are you going to watch my house again?" he said as he got out. "I'll flick the lights. We could have a code or something."

"Like junior spies, right? No, I'm going straight home. I'm pretty sure Mom's waiting for me, and I may as well get it over with."

Will looked at his house. "Yeah." He leaned back in. "Is it too soon to say I love you?"

"Much too soon."

"Then what do I say?"

"Good night."

⇥⇤

She was waiting in the kitchen. Normally we're very careful about hanging our car keys on some hooks on a wall by the back door. Tonight I tossed mine onto the table. They skidded noisily across the slick surface. I kicked off my shoes. They each hit hard against a wall. "Go ahead," I said. "I can tell that you're about to burst."

"He's the boy we saw at the lake Christmas Day. You found him."

"Yes."

"He's friends with those kids who died."

"No. He didn't know them."

That puzzled her. "He seemed so upset that day."

I made a quick decision. "He's the unidentified jogger who found her body."

If a person can collapse without moving, she did it just then. It was like she was suddenly soft and empty. When she'd recovered a bit, I explained about my website and how he found me at the store.

"You met only last night?" Her voice was still weak, but clearly regaining strength.

"Yes."

"Hanna . . ." My name slid out of her throat like a sigh. "Your bedroom door was open. I couldn't help seeing . . ." Her voice gave out.

"A messy room? It gets that way. Please, Mom, don't assume things, okay?"

Obviously, she wasn't convinced. She tapped on the table and chewed her lip. More was coming. Big breath, shoulders back, mustering strength—yes, here it comes.

"I realize that the terrible tragedy of those children dying is a very intense thing, especially for him, poor boy. But Hanna, it just wouldn't be emotionally healthy to get too close to soon. In fact, it would probably doom any potential long-term relationship."

"Thanks for the advice. I'll keep it in mind."

Not charmed by my tone, she narrowed her eyes. The tapping increased in pace, then stopped as she folded her hands. "That you might be precipitously and prematurely intimate with that boy isn't my only concern about the relationship."

"That boy's name is Will. And what else bugs you?"

"How old is he?"

"What?" The word came out as half laugh, half gasp.

She nodded vigorously, as if confirming something. "Fourteen, I'd say."

"You're nuts."

She wagged a finger at me. "I have worked with teenage boys for sixteen years. Don't tell me I can't pin an age on one the moment I meet him. Will's physically mature for the most part—"

All parts, I thought.

"—but those eyes, his manner, his sweet sad beard. Oh,

Hanna, maybe fifteen, but just barely. How old is he?"

"I don't know exactly. He hasn't said. I assumed—"

Which was the wrong thing to say. Her eyebrows shot up, capping a righteous smirk.

"He did say he wasn't eighteen *yet*. He goes to South and takes math classes at the U, and I . . ." Oh, man. Time for a deep breath. In, out. "I *assumed* he meant he was doing post-secondary and that he was about my age or a year younger. Okay, I do know he's not a senior. He said that." And not much more, I realized, thinking about it.

Mom said, "Miriam Weidt down the block is taking accelerated math classes at the U and she's twelve. Honey, you get that it would be wrong, don't you, to be so close to someone that young?"

"Twelve? You bet it's too young."

She slapped the table, giving a clear direction: *Cut it out, Hanna*.

I rose. "I think you're wrong, Mom. I'll ask him tomorrow. I'm tired. I'm going to bed."

In my room I sat down on the desk chair and stared at the disheveled bed. Fourteen?

No rule, of course, against younger boyfriends, but still. Fourteen?

An hour later, when I heard the TV go off downstairs and heard Mom climb the stairs and walk to her room, I was still sitting in the chair and staring at the bed.

Fourteen?

Mom wiped a slow-moving drop of heavy cream off the side of her coffee mug with her thumb. "What are you doing?" she asked. She licked the thumb.

"Going out."

"Hanna, it's Sunday. We never go out." She set the mug down on the counter. "Where exactly are you going?"

When I didn't answer, but just stood silently at the back door with the car keys in one hand and my left shoe in the other, she exhaled impressively. Whoa, Mom. I wouldn't have guessed even a veteran dancer (much less one twenty years past her dancing prime) had that much lung capacity.

That big a sigh deserved an answer. "Will's house."

"It can't wait?"

I shook my head and pulled on the shoe.

"It's only nine. He won't be up. His family won't be up. They might be at church. It's rude to just drop in."

"I'm not going to bother his family. He gets up early to run and he should be back by now."

"Hanna, please don't go. Whatever it is you think you have to say to him can wait. This is our day. I want it." When I didn't reply, she pointed to the phone. "If it's that important, just call him."

I shook my head. I didn't want to catch him in a room with his family. Even more important, I wanted to see his face when I heard his answer. "I'll be back soon," I said as I hurried out the door.

⤜✦⤛

The lawyer sister was coming out the side door as I approached Will's house. She stopped at the bottom of the steps, put her hands on her hips, and waited for me. "You're Will's friend," she said flatly, as if the statement were the opening of some courtroom exam.

"For the record, yes," I replied. She tilted her head a bit as she laughed and her floppy purple hat threatened to slide off her dark red hair. A purple hat, with that hair color? She wore a bright yellow jacket that looked as if it had come from a thrift shop Dumpster. Obviously she and Will had learned how to dress from the same source. "I'd like to talk to your brother. Would you mind asking him to come out?"

As she considered my request, she looked for a while at the house, then back at me. Suddenly she moved, linking her arm through mine and hauling me toward the steps. "Please," I protested, "I'd rather talk to him out here."

She was quite a bit shorter than me, but sturdy—the kind of physique my mom calls a fireplug. As she dragged me, I moved forward with tripping little steps. "He's still out running," she said. "You can wait inside. I'm going for bagels." She finally let go of my arm as she went up the steps to open the door. "What kind do you like?" Without waiting for an answer she shouted into the house, "Everybody decent? Will's friend is here."

Obviously I was quickly approaching the abyss of total humiliation. However, not for nothing am I the daughter of the world's best drama teacher. I stood tall, lowered my voice, and said, "Look—"

And then I did. Will's dad and other sister stood at the door.

"Holy cow," I said. "I'm going to kill him."

⇥⇤

Aerin Walker handed me a huge mug of coffee. Before she sat at the kitchen table she tightened the drawstring of her baggy flannel pajama pants, tugged her faded sweatshirt down over her hips, and then ran both hands through shaggy dark curls. She pushed a carton of cream across the table. There was an unfinished jigsaw puzzle spread out, and the carton plowed through the scattered pieces as it came to me. "You'll want this. My sister makes pretty thick coffee. So tell me: Who did you recognize first—the congressman or the reclusive, tragic singer?"

I took a long time to dose the very dark coffee. When I finished, I picked up a puzzle piece and immediately set it in place in the picture. "Your dad."

"Ah, good answer. And then you knew who I was. Little brother hadn't told you, thus the surprise."

I nodded. "Yeah." I looked at Will's father. Like Beth the lawyer, he was a fireplug, shorter than me by an inch or two. Like both his daughters, he'd obviously rolled out of bed and decided to go with thrift shop casual. He was in a long-sleeved green T-shirt, baggy blue sweats, old plaid slippers. Reading glasses hung from a pink cord around his neck. His mostly gray hair was cropped into a brush cut. As he leaned against the sink and stared at me with a slight smile, I pasted on a wide smile for the member of Congress from Minnesota's Fifth District. "I voted for you last November, sir. So did everyone I know, actually, but then you always win easily, don't you?"

That wiped the smile right off his face. Which puzzled me—I mean, I'd just told a politician he'd gotten my vote and lots of others, so why was he unhappy?

He sat down next to me. "Hanna, you've voted? How old are you?"

Oh, damn. Well, that was all I needed to know. You win, Mom. "Eighteen. I'm a senior at Humphrey."

He sat back and looked at the ceiling for help.

Aerin gave a throaty, country-yokel chuckle into her

mug: *Heh heh heh*. Not a pretty sound. Hearing that sort of noise—no way in the world you'd figure her producing silky rich vocals in any band, much less one that had won five Grammys and had a mega-hit CD.

I started to speak. How do you properly address a congressman? "Your Honor—"

Aerin laughed again. Her dad looked at her unhappily, then leaned forward with his hands clasped on the table. I glanced away and spotted another puzzle piece I knew I could place. My fingers tapped on my thighs.

" 'Mr. Walker' is fine," he said. "Hanna, I realize that you and Will have just met, and so there's probably nothing to be worried about, but you know, don't you, that he's a freshman at South? He's fourteen."

"No," I said weakly, staring at the table. "He didn't tell me that either." I looked at Mr. Walker. "But it doesn't matter because we're just friends." Not exactly a lie, because from that moment on Will and I were just friends. At least until I killed him.

Relieved, Will's dad smiled and got up from the table, turning toward the coffeepot. Aerin leaned close to me. "Fourteen," she whispered. "Jailbait."

Without turning around, the congressman said, "Cork it, Aerin."

I took a good look at her, steady and long enough to make her smile disappear. "He talked a bit about Beth," I said, "but he never mentioned you by name. Not surprising, I guess. He did say he had two sisters. One a lawyer, the other a writer who worked for an ad agency. That's you?"

"He wasn't lying." She took a sip from her mug and made a face. "Smartest girl in the world, my big sister.

Done with law school at twenty-two and only two years later she's heading up a whole section at her firm. Did he tell you that? No? Well, obviously there's lots he skipped over. Anyway, she's smart but she cannot make coffee. Yes, I'm a writer—a songwriter, as you probably know. And, yes, I do some freelance work now for an ad agency. You should hear the potato chip jingle I just finished." She watched my face carefully. "Yeah, I know—pretty sad."

I turned to Will's father. "All he said about his dad was that you were a lawyer and out of town a lot."

"All true, but obviously not the whole story." He started making a fresh pot of coffee.

"You can't blame him, really," Aerin said. Our eyes met again. She seemed so familiar. How long had it been since her face was all over the news—two years?

Wait until Mom heard about this: Aerin Walker.

She took my silence as argument. "Okay, maybe you can blame him a little, but the boy just wanted to be sure you liked him for him."

The boy. I looked at the puzzle and quickly placed three more pieces. Aerin whistled. "Wow. How do you do it? All that monotonous white and blue."

"It's not monotonous, especially the clouds." I held up a piece. "See the shading? I bet it goes in the corner by you." I tossed it to her. She picked it up and frowned as she turned it around and around. I took it from her hands and snapped it into place, then stood. "I'm sorry I dropped in like this. My mom told me it was a rude thing to do, but I ignored her."

Aerin held up another puzzle piece and made a face.

"What do you mean, rude? We just love unexpected company early on Sunday morning. And you shouldn't leave now, Hanna, because I think it's about to get very interesting." She tipped her head toward the next room just as her mother appeared.

"Well," the woman said as she walked into the kitchen, "company." She yawned. "Thought I heard a strange voice."

I sat back down.

"This is Will's friend Hanna Martin, the one who has the website," Aerin said.

"Hello, Mrs. Walker," I mumbled.

"Uh-uh," Aerin said. "She goes by *Miz* Callahan. Mom, you should see her go to work on this puzzle."

Will's mom took the seat his dad had left. She twisted around, motioning toward the coffee, which gave me a chance to check her out. Tall, with beautifully highlighted wavy red hair cut very short. Baggy old pajama pants, faded T-shirt, worn-out slippers. Did the whole family forage in the same sad laundry pile?

Ms. Callahan's unsmiling pale blue eyes quickly pinned me in place. Neither of us looked away. An ice queen, I wondered, or a fierce mother lion? Was I about to get a lecture on leaving young boys—her young boy—alone? Or maybe a reprimand about amusing myself with a website filled with ghoulish, voyeuristic drawings. She was obviously charging batteries before slamming me with something.

She looked away briefly when her husband handed her his mug. "Beth got down first," he said. "I'm making a fresh pot."

Will's mom sipped, made a face, and set down the

mug. She picked up a puzzle piece and snapped it in place. Aerin made an annoyed sound. "You had some interesting things on your site, Hanna," Ms. Callahan said. "Thank you for sending the one of Will. Tell me—the red was light, right, and not blood, like he thinks?"

"Not blood," I said.

A smile briefly appeared, then faded. "Those pictures of . . . you must have known that young couple. I'm so sorry."

Obviously Will had kept his promise and not told my secret. "I didn't know them," I said. "But I live near the lake and walk there all the time. It's a terrible thing and hard not to think about and I tend to draw what I think about."

"So," Aerin said, "I guess that means you think about my brother. Mom, Hanna's a senior at Humphrey; she voted for Dad." When her mother made a sharp sound, Aerin added cheerily, "Don't worry, she and Will are just friends. She says."

"Aerin . . ." her dad said wearily.

I looked down at the table. I should have left long ago. Weird thing was, in spite of the cut-it-with-a-knife tension, I didn't want to leave the sunny kitchen where soon everyone would be eating bagels and drinking decent coffee and talking and making slow progress on the puzzle.

My family's close. We don't let a lot of outsiders in, not like we used to, but anyone who gets near us tends to get sucked in pretty good.

Not like we used to. I glanced at Will's famous sister. No wonder.

I wanted to stay so I could be part of it all. I wanted to

see Will's face when he walked in. And maybe I wanted to stay because I had my own surprise to lay on them.

I fixed another puzzle piece. Ms. Callahan made an admiring little sound. She rose and stood by her husband. I looked at them standing face-to-face exchanging god knows what telepathic message. "Holy cow," I murmured as I watched them look at each other. "Put the two of you in a jar, shake it up, and out comes Will."

"That's pretty much what happened," Aerin said, "except it didn't take place in a jar."

I rose and said, "Cork it, Aerin." Her parents laughed.

She lifted her mug. "Touché, Hanna."

I opened the door, then paused. Cold air rushed in and I shut it again. "Since it's a day for springing surprises—"

"Springing surprises," Aerin echoed. "Nice phrase."

"I've got one too. My mom's name is Claudia Martin. She teaches at—"

Before I could finish, Aerin let loose a long, low laugh. I glanced at her parents. They'd both paled, and she'd put a hand on his shoulder, as if to steady herself.

"Yeah," I said. "Just so you know."

Aerin said, "*What* a co-ink-ee-dink."

"Yeah," I said again.

She got up, walked over, and hugged me. "That's for her, okay? And tell her hi. No, wait, tell her hi *and* thanks."

"Aerin," her father cautioned yet again.

"I'm not being snotty; I mean it," she said. "And don't you two want to send a belated grateful greeting to the first teacher with nerve enough to tell the congressman and his wife how messed up their daughter was? C'mon, Mom and Dad—it's been eight years, so don't you think it's time we thanked Dr. Martin?"

"Uh-uh," I said. "Off campus, she goes by *Miz* Martin." I nodded to Will's parents and left the house.

I'd only reached the bottom step when the door opened. Aerin came out and pulled it shut behind her. She'd slipped into pink velour flip-flops, but wore no coat. Wind whipped her curls around.

"Jeez, you look like Will," I said.

"You think? People usually say I'm my mom's clone, except for the hair color, but I could never see it. You look at things carefully, don't you?"

I nodded.

"Ever get you in trouble?"

I nodded.

"Yeah, tell me about it. I really used to—" The door opened behind her. She rolled her eyes.

"Aerin," said her mom, "what are you doing? You'll freeze."

"No, Mother," she said crisply. "I will not freeze. I assure you that I'm still sane enough to come inside before I freeze. I want to talk to Hanna, okay?"

The door closed.

Aerin smiled at me. "I am freezing, but there's no way I'm going in now, not for at least a minute."

"How old are you?"

"Almost twenty-three. Yeah, I know—too old to be acting this way. But my arrested development is not what I wanted to talk about. It's Will. I don't buy the just-friends bit. I watched you guys say good night last night. And I also noticed that he came home with bed hair and his shirt on backwards."

I took my time pulling on my gloves. Let her get cold.

"Don't get too mad that he didn't tell you about us. He's been so protective of me ever since the accident." She waited, watching.

I nodded to show that I knew what she was talking about. Of course, the whole world knew.

"Lots of people try to get to Dad or me through the rest of the family, but because he's the youngest, he gets it especially hard."

"Hiding you and your dad is not what I'm mad about. I understand that he'd want to do that. But he led me on about how old he was. He let me believe he was older."

She hugged herself. Wind howled, and snow whipped about. Someone pushed aside the blinds over the door window. "Hanna, you must have figured out that he's absolutely crazy about you," Aerin said. "The kid has been floating for two days now, and not just because you two . . ." Her head rocked from side to side.

"He told you?"

She smiled. "No, but it was easy enough to guess. Trust me: That he got laid by an interesting older girl is not why he's been so happy. Okay, of course it is, but just partly. Considering how really blue he was after that whole scene with finding the body, his complete turn-around in mood—" The door opened slightly and she quickly yanked it closed.

Enough frozen bodies. "It's cold," I said. "I'm going. Nice to meet you."

"Fine. We won't talk about Will. That's not the only reason I came after you. I meant it about giving your mom that message. I suppose it didn't sound that way inside. I'm sincere. She might not believe it, but I figured out long ago that getting kicked out of Whipple was a good thing. And the lecture she laid on Mom and Dad the day it happened really woke them up. She's probably told you all about it."

"She never talks about her students' private business and I've learned not to ask. Even . . ." I shook my head.

She smiled. "Even when it's a juicy story about someone famous. But you obviously knew I had a history with her, so she must have said something."

"Nothing, ever. I suppose I read something in a magazine after . . ." I shrugged.

Aerin blew on her hands. "After the accident, you mean. Lots of that magazine stuff was wrong. You need to know, then, that I never actually punched her like it said in *Rolling Stone*. I tried, but she was too quick."

"She is quick."

"Tell her I said she can tell you anything about me and Whipple. And tell her hi."

I said, "Go inside."

She stepped down and kissed me on the cheek. "Nice to meet you, Hanna Martin. By the way, he runs along the river road. He cuts back over on Twenty-fourth. Let him down easy, okay? He's the only brother I've got and, anyway, in a few years you might want—"

Her mother couldn't wait any longer. She opened the door, walked out, and fastened a hand on Aerin's arm. "Nice to meet you, Hanna; please come by again," Ms. Callahan said as she hauled her laughing daughter up the steps and into the house.

><

I saw him before he saw me. As soon as the yellow cap came into view, I bolted from my parked car and ran. I'm not sure he even saw me coming. I don't suppose under normal circumstances I could have tackled him, but the sidewalk was slick in spots and I was steaming and when I slammed into him, he flew backwards. My feet went out from under me too, and I landed on top of him. I pounded his chest. "You son of a bitch, you're only fourteen! I had sex with a fourteen-year-old boy! I could go to jail!"

He pulled the cap down over his eyes.

I'd taken in too much cold air; my lungs pinched. I sat on the snow and wiped my runny nose with the back of my glove. Will lifted the cap, saw my face, and pulled it back down.

"I should have figured it out," I said. "My mother figured it out the moment she saw you in the kitchen. You lied to me, Will. You said, 'I'll have another year at South.' Right. Another year and then *two more* after that. You let me believe—" I had to catch my breath.

"You believed exactly what you wanted to believe." He sat up, pushing the cap back from his eyes.

"I hate you, Will."

He blew out air. "I knew that was coming. But now that I actually hear you say it, I guess I don't really believe it."

We breathed heavily in tandem. He'd done seven miles; I'd run seven yards.

"No, I don't hate you," I said finally. "But you are dead to me. Got it? I am so furious with you. You are dead to me."

"C'mon, Hanna. You saw what you wanted to see and I—"

"And you figured you had a sure thing. Typical guy." But he wasn't typical, which was what had blinded me from the start.

He peeled off his cap and held it between his hands. Hair blew around his face. "I didn't figure anything like that and you know it. Now who's not being honest? Don't be changing things around now just because you're mad. I loved being with you and you loved being with me and we both loved finally talking about that whole nightmare. The sex just seemed right, like it was the first right thing to happen. It was like both of us needed to hold on to something because so much else was going wrong."

Oh hell. I set my head against his shoulder. Fourteen, I thought. How cruel can life be?

"I told you we should have run away," he said softly.

I pulled back. "Maybe so, because that would have made sleeping together only the second-dumbest thing we did."

"It wasn't wrong."

"Fine for you to say. You're not the one who could be hauled off to jail."

"They have no idea what happened, okay? And even if they did, my parents would never make that sort of trouble for you. If you met them, you'd know that."

"I have met them. *And* Aerin *and* Beth. I went to your house to talk to you and ended up sitting in the kitchen visiting with the family. Well, not so much Beth; she left to get bagels. I think I like your family. I'm sorry I blew the chance to know them. I can never face your parents again. And don't be so sure they haven't guessed what happened. My mother figured it out, and Aerin thought it was pretty obvious."

He twisted the cap.

"Aerin said you were protective. I think that's sweet,

Will. I understand why you wouldn't want to talk about them to someone you'd just met. And now I also understand completely why Beth told you to get the hell out of the park once you found the body."

He shifted and made space between us.

"I told my mom that you were the unidentified jogger. I'm sorry."

"I didn't ask you to keep my secret."

"I promise it won't go any further. It must be really hard being part of a public family." I pushed up and stood. "I like you so much, but I cannot have a fourteen-year-old boyfriend, especially one I slept with by mistake."

"It wasn't a mistake," he said. When I didn't answer, he added, "We can be friends, right?"

"Will, I absolutely can't see you again." I took a few steps, then turned back around. "You don't have to keep my secret. You can tell your family that I talked to those kids."

I'd almost reached the car when I heard snow crunch behind me. I turned just as he caught up. He looked down.

Oh, god. He seemed so young.

He still held the yellow cap. Suddenly he tugged it down on my head until it covered my ears. Will whispered something and ran away.

→←

Hadn't she moved?

Mom sat at the table looking at a spot on the wall.

I stuffed the hat in a coat pocket, hung the car keys, and slipped off my shoes. I dropped my coat over a chair. "You were right. You win. I'm not going to see him again."

Her voice was weak. "I don't feel like I've won any-thing. Darling, I think—"

I hushed her with a raised hand. "I will tell you every-thing A to Z, but only if you don't tell me what you think and you don't make me go see Ray again."

"I don't know if I can make either of those promises."

"Fine. I'm going to my room." Would her curiosity be too much?

Yes.

She grabbed my hand. "All right, Hanna. I will trust you to take measure of things. If you don't think you need to see Ray and if you really don't want my input, then I accept that. I think the important thing is for you to talk."

So, I talked. I started with waiting for Spencer in the airport and went through it all.

The rough part was telling her about talking to Derek and Lindsey. When I'd finished with that, she called a break. She made toast and scrambled eggs for us to eat while I continued.

She was amused by my pretend-grandmother and the ass-covering swimsuits and she loved hearing about Will reading to the kids in the store.

I skipped over the sex.

"But here's the clincher," I said as I spread jam over my last square of toast. "His dad's Mark Walker, our con-gressman. Which I didn't know until I got to the house this morning. Another minor detail Will chose not to mention."

Her fork froze halfway to her mouth. She made the family connection immediately. "Aerin?"

I nodded.

"That poor girl. Was she there? Did you meet her? I'd heard she'd moved back home."

"I met the whole family."

Mom wasn't interested in the whole family, just her former student. "How did she seem to you?"

"On edge, maybe. Kind of caustic. At least in front of her parents."

"Everything was finally going so well for her, then that horrible accident."

"She says hi and thanks." Mom looked startled. "I think she meant it. She said it turned out to be a good thing that she got kicked out of Whipple and that her parents needed the lecture you gave them."

"I did not ever lecture her parents. We met just once and . . ." Mom shook her head, not pleased with the memory. "I never got to know the family because she was only at Whipple a few months her freshman year. I do remember that there was a younger brother I never met." She looked at me. "Much younger."

"About eight years younger," I said, stuffing my mouth with toast. "Like you thought, he's fourteen."

She made a soft noise. "To think of him finding the girl's body. I'm rather surprised we didn't hear about that. Even if he's a minor, I cannot believe the media would leave that alone—another child of Congressman Walker found on the scene with a corpse. That's simply too juicy a story." She glared at some unseen foe, another fierce mother lion protecting the young.

"We didn't hear about it because not even the police know who reported the body. He left the scene just so there wouldn't be those stories. We can't ever tell, Mom, okay? I promised him that."

"Never," she said, nodding. Then: "Oh, honey. Look at you."

Yeah, look at me. I'd started, finally, to cry.

She wrapped her arms around me and rocked as buckets of pent-up tears flowed. The hug felt so good until she started talking. "How heavy it must all seem, darling. I'm sure you've burdened yourself with enormous guilt."

I pulled away. "Stop it, Mom; you promised. I don't want to hear it." I wiped my cheeks. "Besides, you're wrong. That's not what it is. It's not the guilt." I wiped my nose with my sleeve. "The thing is, I just really like him."

>‹

I was still in the kitchen, sitting numbly at the table and watching Mom load the dishwasher when the phone rang. Mom checked the ID. "Maura," she said, and we exchanged puzzled looks.

"She knows better than to call on Sunday," I said.

"Better see what she wants," Mom said.

"Thank god you picked up," Maura blurted as soon as I answered the phone. "I've left about three messages on your cell."

"What's wrong?"

"I've dug up something really big and I needed to tell you about it right away. That's why I busted in on your Sunday."

"Details?"

"I found the guy with the hat. I haven't met him or anything but I know who he is. It took this long because he goes to South, but boy oh boy. First of all, forget about him. He's only—"

"Maura, stop." I smiled at Mom, shrugged, and took the phone into the living room.

"I hate to break it to you, Hanna, but he's only a freshman. Gorgeous, apparently. He played baseball with Chad last summer. He must be good because he got invited to play in the top league with older guys. That's how I tracked him down, through Chad. We talked at church this morning. That's not who told me he was gorgeous, though. That was Megan; she was with Chad, can you believe it? That seems like a big step, to go to church with someone. Anyway, his name's Will Walker and his—"

"Maura, I know. Will and I met the other night. And I know who his dad is and I know who his sister is. I met them both about an hour ago."

"You did?" There was a satisfied sigh. "How messed up is she?"

"I don't want to talk about it."

She did. "*Rolling Stone* did an update on the anniversary of the crash last year and it said she's a total recluse now, but then, wouldn't you be? I mean, god, to go through that nightmare, to be the driver in a horrible accident and everyone else in the band dies but you don't, and to make it worse the next thing you know every magazine in the world gets to run pictures of you crying and cradling a dead and bloody body by the wreck just because some asshole in the next car has a camera and shoots pictures instead of helping. I mean, after all that, you'd be a total mess."

"We didn't really get around to talking about it."

"Can you introduce me? I still play their CD pretty often. Too bad they only had time to make one."

"Maura, I'll probably never see her again. I met her and we chatted for a while, but that's not info to share, okay?

Talk and you die. We're at that level on this subject. I'm absolutely not saying anything about her. See you in school tomorrow."

><

My heart wasn't into it, but I muddled through the rest of the Sunday rituals. Finally, after too much silence, Mom gave up and left to go to the hospital and see Charles's new grandson. I went to my room. I put Will's hat on Roscoe, my oldest and favorite stuffed animal. "One elephant," I whispered, tapping the bear's chest.

I ran my fingers up the spines of CD cases until I found the one I wanted. Chinook.

It had a typical photo on the insert. The four band members all wore thrift shop clothes and were posed with plenty of attitude. Aerin at least looked like she got the joke.

Oh help: She stood with her weight on one hip and her hands slipped into back pockets. Just like Will.

I put the disc on the player. For a while a couple of years ago everyone was playing either this CD or the *One Night* soundtrack, which had two great Chinook songs. The music was hard to classify. Alt-country sure, but it wouldn't be wrong to call it Blue-Eyed Blues either. Whatever the label, the music was loaded with witty lyrics, raise-the-roof instrumentals, tight four-part harmonies.

Four part.

And then there was one.

4
Talk and You Die

I've always liked high school. I'm not deluded, of course. I know these aren't the best years of my life, but as a subject and experience, it's pretty interesting.

The cafeteria, for example. Like any student who stays out of major trouble, I got open lunch privileges junior year and I don't have to eat in the building, but usually I do. I brown-bag my meal, naturally; that's required for survival. So if I don't eat the food, and if most of my friends are out exercising their privilege to leave, why do I stick it out? Well, what can I say: I like sitting in the middle of chaos.

And I mean the middle. The first day of sophomore year I came in early and walked it off. Best I could measure by that crude system, the center of the Humphrey High cafeteria is the serving-counter end of the fourth table in the center row.

On the even calendar days I sit on the north side of the table. Odd days, the south. Either place: the middle of chaos.

That's where I was when Maura and Kelsey found me on Monday.

They both do post-secondary in the mornings, driving together to classes at a nearby community college, then returning to the high school for choir and AP physics. Today they both looked as if they'd run straight in from the parking lot to some life and death emergency.

Maura slid into a seat across from me. "What is going on? What the hell has been happening with you and why didn't we know? I want to hear about Aerin Walker!"

I glanced around and noticed a sophomore sitting at the table who was staring at us. "Not here, okay?" I said softly to Maura. "This isn't the place." No lie—there must have been six hundred kids in the room. And while the din made it fairly safe for talking, there were at least five people within earshot, and that was four more than you needed to guarantee a secret would spread. True, the five trying to tune in to what we were saying were all under-classmen and had been clueless middle schoolers two years ago when a speeding Cadillac SUV hit ice, spun out of control, rolled across the freeway median, and slammed Aerin's car into the front end of a semi. The way fame flashes for only an instant, these kids might not even know her name.

Maura leaned forward, bursting with questions. I held up a hand to hush her.

My secret to lunch period survival: I always have a

stack of coloring books and a large container of crayons. Anyone is welcome to sit at my table—and trust me, everybody calls it Hanna's Table—but only if they color and limit the chitchat. Need I say that it's the calmest place in the room?

I scanned the books remaining in the stack and then handed *Porky Pig Goes West* to Maura. "Hanna," she said, "at least tell us—"

I shook my head. I wasn't talking. Not here, maybe not anywhere or anytime. She again opened her mouth. I said, "Cork it, Maura." She made a face, but fished around in the crayon container, found a sweet blue, and started in on Porky.

Kelsey picked up a handful of crayons and rolled them between her palms. I shot her a look and she rolled her eyes and put all but one back as she reached for *Bob the Builder*.

After I put the finishing touches on page seven of *Sleeping Beauty Barbie,* I glanced at the clock and stood— the signal for everyone at the table to turn things in.

Once we were out of the lunchroom Kelsey said calmly, "You really met Aerin Walker and weren't going to tell us?"

Last night I'd told Maura not to talk, but she knew, as I knew, that the threat didn't include spilling it all to Kelsey. I may have laid down the Talk and You Die warning, but that was for outsiders. That's just how it is with the three of us.

"I met her, but her brother's the real story." That should have distracted them, but no. Obviously I couldn't get them off Aerin.

Maura persisted. "What's she like?"

Okay. We were best friends, and at that level of friendship you don't tight-lip this major a story one hundred percent. I'd have to share something. "She's nice. Sarcastic. Thin. She needs a good haircut. She's concerned about her brother because he's younger than me and we got a little too close a little too fast. And that's all I'm going to say about her. By the way, he's dead to me."

We reached the music room door. I don't sing, but I know most everyone in choir and I chatted with people as they headed into class. I finally turned to Maura and Kelsey and said, "I just don't feel right talking about her, maybe because I have the feeling she's not totally healthy. End of conversation. See you."

Maura grabbed my hand. "Okay, then what about the brother? How did you track him down? What do you mean by too close too fast—the obvious?"

Major rule of keeping best friends: Don't sit on too many secrets. Otherwise, why be friends? "Can I tell you something that I'm not proud of?"

"You didn't! That fast?" Maura said. "And with a freshman?"

I shook my head. "That's not it. Well, okay; it's part of the story." I stepped closer and lowered my voice. "First of all, though, he found me. And yes, we did—first night, even. But you should also know that at that point I had no idea who he was related to and I definitely had no idea how young he was. I just got swept away because he's very sweet and very sexy. But that's not what I was going to tell you."

"What, then?" Kelsey said. Her voice was calm, but her eyes had widened. She put a restraining hand on Maura, who was again starting to speak.

"The couple that went through the ice and died right before Christmas? I think I was the last person they talked to. I was down there that night. I'd gone out for a walk, and they came by on that ATV. It was loud and horrible and they were so obnoxious. She threw a condom at me and told me to go find someone to use it with. I got pissed. And now for the last few weeks no matter what I do I can't get it out of my head that maybe I could have stopped them from going out on the lake. I knew the ice was thin in spots. Some skiers had just come by and told me but I didn't say anything because I was pissed." I dared a glance at them. They were both stunned. "What's almost as bad is that apparently I'm the only person in the world who knew that right before they died they were on the verge of a huge fight."

Kelsey gasped. "Their funeral. That's why you—" Mrs. Evenson, the choir director, called to Maura and Kelsey. The halls had quieted and emptied. Shit, now I'd get another tardy from math class.

I nodded. "Yeah. That's why I thought it sucked." I shifted the coloring books from one arm to another and walked away. I called over my shoulder, "Talk and you die."

⇥⇤

Mom had started auditions and tech work for *Our Town* and wouldn't be leaving school until late. After I got home from a three-hour shift of flattering swimsuit shoppers I made a dinner of peanut butter toast and grapefruit juice and then went to my room. I checked for messages on the house phone: three after-school calls from Maura and two from Kelsey, about the same number as had piled up on my cell. I didn't call either of them. For one thing, I knew that at that moment Kelsey was in the middle of a hockey game and Maura was in the stands cheering. And besides, I'd said all I wanted to.

I should have studied, but, like most nights, I pulled out the drawing paper, clipped a few sheets to the easel, sharpened my pencils, and got lost.

Before I knew what I was doing, I'd marked a faint grid on the paper. A room appeared. Window over a sink. Table and chairs. Coffeemaker. People: one at a table, two by the sink.

I yanked the sheet off the easel, balled it up, and tossed it in the waste basket. I stared at the next sheet, then began again, pulling the lens of the camera eye in closer, focusing on the person at the table. Her hand hovered over pieces of a puzzle.

I like drawing scenes. Maybe that comes from working with Mom. Each one is like a glimpse of a moment in an unscripted play—something has happened, but what, exactly? And even more interesting—what happens next?

Another try. And another. Again—yes, this one. The camera's eye has moved in even more. Aerin comes into focus. Huh. I think I've made her plainer than she is. Gaunt. Oh crap, her eyes are no good. Too round, like those Keane paintings with the doe-eyed children. I erased the eyes and tried again. Oh, great, Hanna: Now you've given her *his* eyes. Large and dark.

I sat back, remembering those eyes looking at me and memorizing everything they could see.

I erased the eyes again, but this time I'd turned the eraser and used a soiled spot. The rubbing left smudged dark sockets.

A face with no eyes is a horrible thing.

→←

The face with no eyes followed me into sleep, appearing at windows and in mirrors and emerging from behind curtains of the dressing rooms at the store. Caught in a time-warped dream world, I raced through a nonsensical

Day in the Life, chased everywhere by multiple faces with no eyes.

When the dream shifted to the lake—as my dreams now almost always did—the face rolling around in the water was a blank white oval, a ghoulish twin to the girl on shore who lay rigid and still in the arms of a tall yellow-capped boy with two smudged sockets on his pale bearded face.

><

I gave Zak an apologetic smile. "I need her for a minute."

He tapped two fingers against his lips and touched them against Kelsey's cheek. He picked up his backpack and walked away. Kelsey dumped her armload of books into the locker and pulled out a gym bag. "I take it you're not avoiding us now."

"Who says I was before?"

She rolled her eyes. "You didn't pick up the phone last night and today you hid during lunch."

"I wasn't hiding. I was in the media center listening to German tapes. Maura found me there. We talked."

Kelsey nodded as she stared at the contents of her locker. "So she said. I'm surprised you're here. I thought she was dropping you off at Whipple. Aren't you picking out paint for the stage or something like that?"

"Headed that way. Maura's with Stricker, clearing up that missing grade."

One of her hockey teammates ran down the hall, batted Kelsey's shoulder, and ran on. "I need to go, Hanna. I've got to give a rousing pep talk before practice."

"Oh, yeah, I forgot. Tough game last night. What is it—your first loss in two years?"

An impatient sigh escaped her. "Hanna, what's up? You

didn't send Zak away because you wanted to console me. You're a great friend, but you've never paid much attention to my hockey games."

True. "Are you still into dreams?"

That surprised her. "Not so much. It was just all so elusive. Why do you ask?" She spun her lock and smiled sideways at me. "Having weird ones about little boys?"

"Funny, but no. Faces with no eyes. Ever come across an explanation for that?"

She cringed. "Yuck. No. And there never is a straight explanation for anything, which is what I hated. It's all about figuring it out on your own and deciding what it is that you want something to mean. Not exactly a science."

"That's no help."

She shrugged. "Like I said, too elusive. Gotta run." She took two steps, then turned back, her blond ponytail swinging in a wide arc. "Were you drawing right before you went to bed?"

I nodded.

"That's all you need to know, Hanna: Don't. It gives you bad dreams."

I don't envy Kelsey's strong, zero-fat body, her Hollywood looks, her 1580 SAT score. I do, though, sometimes envy the matter-of-fact way she handles things. If something doesn't work, fix it. There's always a right answer and a clear path.

As for me, I may have still been drawing in bold colors, but more and more these days when I closed my eyes, I saw a world of shadows.

>‹

I beat Maura to the car. I'd spent most of the last two periods of school staring out the window and watching snow come down; now there was nearly an inch of fresh powder coating the car. I wiped a window with my arm, then swore as the snow fell on my shoes.

Maura came up behind me and unlocked the door as I knocked the snow off my feet.

As we waited for the car to warm, I blew on my hands. "Get the grade fixed?" I asked, though I was sure that Stricker, a passive first-year teacher fresh out of college, couldn't possibly have withstood Maura's energy force.

"No problem. The guy never knew what hit him. I mean, have you seen his desk? He has no system at all for keeping track of things. I know I handed back the test. I know he gave me an A. I shouldn't suffer because he didn't record the grade. Should I hang around at Whipple to give you a ride home?"

"I'll wait for Mom. Thanks for the ride over, though."

She put the car in gear and pulled out, claiming her right-of-way by hitting the horn as a Lexus zigzagged through vacated parking spaces toward the main exit. "Look at what Brandon's driving now." He laid a heavy hand on his horn, and she gave him the fist of fury as she turned her battered red Prizm onto the street. "Giving you a ride is the least I can do. Kelsey and I were just talking, and we're worried about you."

"Kelsey and *I* were just talking, and she didn't say anything about that."

"Those dreams must have freaked you out. Those faces."

I turned and stared at her. I couldn't have left Kelsey five minutes before Maura showed up at the car. We hit a speed bump and bounced in our seats. She read my face. "She left you and found me at physics. Good thing she did too. She helped persuade Stricker that I was telling the truth. Teachers all trust Kels, have you noticed that?"

"Where have you been? I noticed it in fourth grade, probably the very day she transferred from Hale and got put in our class."

"Anyway, we're both worried, Hanna. First you break up with Spencer—"

I looked out the window. "Breaking up was the best thing I've done all year."

"I won't argue with that, believe me. But then you pull a crazy rebound stunt and hop into bed with a freshman. Even if his sister—"

"For the last time: I didn't know about his age or his sister, okay?"

She adjusted the heater controls. "And to top it all, there's that whole thing about those kids and the lake. I know you're not the world's greatest talker, Hanna, but you shouldn't ever sit on stuff like that. You blew us away yesterday. No wonder you're having freaky dreams. Anyway, we figured out what you need to get over all this."

My window had frosted over. I took off a mitten and scraped a few lines with a fingernail. "What do I need?"

She looked over her shoulder as she changed lanes to avoid getting stuck behind a bus that was slowing at a corner. "A three-alarm party with lots of new guys."

>‹

I had doubts about my friends' prescription for healing; still, I showed up at Kelsey's Saturday night after work. By the time I arrived around nine, the party had definitely reached three-alarm level, which was no small trick, as her parents were both home and the party was dry and weed free.

Kelsey's dad opened the door and waved me in. I avoided the mob in the living room and walked straight to the kitchen. Her mom was pulling a batch of cookies out of the oven as she listened to three girls from the hockey team bitch about league rules. Kelsey's younger brothers were arm wrestling at the kitchen table, getting cheered on by Zak and some other high school guys.

One of the guys with Zak was a stranger to me. He flashed a smile when our eyes met. Okay, here we go: new guy number one. Plenty of new guys, Maura had promised, so there was no need to encourage the first one I encountered with anything more than a smile. Of course, if he followed me out of the kitchen, it was probably some sort of sign. I headed toward the crowded living room.

I wasn't followed. Well, fine. I wasn't necessarily interested in finding a new guy, anyway, because I sincerely doubted that the way to forget someone you liked a lot was to spend time with a less interesting person.

The music was a dance mix and people were dancing. It was a motley crowd drawn from all the major school groups, with plenty of new faces. A couple of friends waved me over, but it suddenly felt like too much work to plow through everyone.

A party can be a solitary place.

"Oh, Hanna," I muttered as I pushed through the dancers toward food, "just cork it."

Fortunately for my ironic and self-pitying mood, Kelsey's mom had made molasses cookies. I grabbed three and took a cup of punch from new guy number two. I sniffed the cup he handed me. "Anything in it?" Alcohol rarely made an appearance at our parties, but with all these new faces, there was no telling what madness might take over, even with Kelsey's parents so obviously hovering.

His eyebrows bobbed a couple of times. "The *punch* is virgin."

Ah, a comedian. Probably a new guy from Maura's improv team. I set down the punch, took a can of pop, and grabbed extra cookies before leaving; as long as this joker was perched here I wouldn't be back.

No sooner had I turned away than I was face-to-face with a girl I'd never seen. I glanced around. Maura and Kelsey really had spread the word; I bet I knew less than half of the people there.

"You're Hanna, right?"

I took a small bite of cookie. I nodded.

She was short and had straight blond hair that grazed her shoulders. She wore tight black jeans and a tight pink turtleneck that should have been creaking the way it was stretched over her exotic-dancer breasts.

I'm thoroughly heterosexual, but I found it hard to keep my eyes on her face.

Someone cranked up the music as she started to speak. She gave her head a little shake, then hooked her hand on my arm and pulled me toward the den. I gave my head a little shake and lumbered along beside her.

The lights were low in the den. Everyone was arranged two by two, watching a video.

"Maybe somewhere else?" I said to the girl in pink. She was gaping at the couples. The devil took over. "Unless," I stretched the word out as I tipped my head toward the busy lovebirds, "*that's* why you asked me to join you. I'm flattered, but I don't even know your name."

Now she gaped at me. "That is not funny."

"So why did you want to talk to me?" I said.

Pink Shirt wagged a finger in my face. "You should not be spreading those lies."

"What lies?"

She took a deep breath. The resulting movement was seismic and it briefly caught the attention of every guy within ten feet. "I go to Brethren," she said. "Derek and Lindsey were friends of some friends of mine. You should not be spreading lies about them."

"What lies?" I repeated, whispering this time.

"That they were having a fight and threw . . ." She licked her lips. "You did not even know them."

I stepped closer. "Who told you?"

"I don't gossip."

"*Who?*"

"It's hateful spreading that kind of trash about two good people you didn't even know." She bumped hard against me as she moved to leave.

I set down my pop and grabbed her arm. She winced and made a little noise. "How did you end up at this party?" I said. "Did Kelsey or Maura invite you?"

She glanced back at the den, where the couples had resumed their low-level coupling. "I wish I never had ended up here. I came with a friend who knew about it. And I don't know anyone named Maura or Kelsey." She marched toward the dark room. "Andrea, I'm leaving," she shouted. "Find a ride."

She cut a swath through the dancers. She dug through the coats piled on a card table in the foyer, found hers, and yanked the front door open. Just before she pulled it behind her, she turned and shot me a furious look.

My eyes skipped around the room until I spotted Maura, who stood with Brian as they chatted with some of the improv team. Kelsey was just beyond her, talking with her parents, who stood near the stairway, apparently about to retreat to a quieter place.

I must have sent out some sort of vibe, because Kelsey and Maura looked at me at the same moment. They both made comical faces when they saw me staring.

Who was it? Which one had breached our years-old trust?

Something fell on my socks. I looked down. I'd crushed the cookies into crumbs.

Maura shouted my name and waved me over. I shook my head. No way I wanted to talk with either of them now. This was not the place. I needed—

"Hanna?"

I looked over my shoulder. Punch Bowl New Guy.
"Yes?"

"Andy Corelli. Hey, why the attitude?"

"Sorry." I emptied the crumbs in my palm into an abandoned punch cup.

The music spiked up again. He leaned in to speak,

steadying himself with a hand on my shoulder. "Someone told me that you live near Uptown."

"*Who* told you?"

He recoiled. "The dad on duty. Look, I didn't mean to bother you. And I'm sorry about the virgin punch joke earlier. I'm spending the weekend with my mom. She just moved into those new condos on Thirty-sixth, near Calhoun. Dad On Duty told me you live in the same neighborhood and that maybe you drove tonight. I could use a ride home when you leave. But if it doesn't work out, that's cool. I'll keep asking around."

Maura's laugh rose above the music. I twisted toward the familiar voice. She and three others were looking at Andy and me. Maura winked.

I turned and said to Andy, "I'm leaving now."

>‹-

As soon as the vents were spewing warm air he unzipped his jacket. "Thanks for the ride. I hate being a new guy at a big party. Don't know why I went except that I didn't want to hang out with my mom. I think she was relieved. She took off with friends even before I was gone." He flipped down the visor and checked the CDs in the holder. "Ah, the Ravonettes. Love this one. We could drive around and listen for a while. I've got some weed."

"Sorry. I worked all day. I'm tired. I don't smoke."

"No problem."

He had made a stupid joke earlier, but at least he was smart enough now to read my mood and keep quiet all the way around the lake. When I turned onto Thirty-sixth he pointed. "It's the brick building with the wide white door." I checked traffic, made a perfect U-turn, and pulled up to the curb by a hydrant. He rubbed his chest as he studied me. "Thanks for the rescue. I'm usually at my dad's in St. Paul, but who knows, maybe I'll like it over here and be around a lot."

I fixed what I hoped was a neutral look on my face and turned so he could see it.

He narrowed his eyes, interpreting. He came to a conclusion and moved in for a kiss. I didn't resist, if only because I knew it couldn't last long, as the gear shift had to be poking his ribs. He pulled back. "Want to come up? Mom's out with girlfriends at a movie. We'd be alone."

"I'm tired."

"That's cool. Another time, maybe. We can make it a real date." He traced my lips with a finger, then let it drop to my chin and travel down my neck. "I'm always interested in a girl who says yes to a little first-night fun. A girl who doesn't mind cutting through the crap."

"What do you mean by that?" I snarled. "Who the hell told you about—" I bit down on my lip hard. Took a moment to calm myself. "Who invited you to the party?"

"Some guy I met in a coffee shop today. We played chess and got to talking."

"Name?"

He tossed his hands up. "I don't know for sure. He introduced himself as Jeremy, but people in the shop called him Stoner."

Jeremy Blackstone. That was no help, though. He was friends with both Zak and Brian.

Andy zipped up his jacket. "Sorry I upset you. Guess I made the wrong move."

I nodded. "Yes. But now you can make the right one." I reached across and opened his door. "Get out."

Maura and Kelsey and I became friends halfway through fourth grade. Since then—not a single fight between any of us. Three friends can pile up a lot of history and a lot of secrets in eight unbroken years together. For as long as we'd been friends, telling something to one or both of the others was as safe as not telling anyone. *Talk and you die*—it was a warning we all used and we all understood.

But now one of them had talked and her boyfriend had talked even more. And suddenly I understood what the familiar old warning really meant.

Talk and the friendship dies.

On Sunday Mom and I were both listless and short with each other. She commented on how much I snacked. I pointed out how anal it was that even on stay-at-home Sundays by ten o'clock she was made up and dressed nice enough for a photo shoot. She vetoed my TiVo choice (a first-season *Friends* episode I'd never seen) and I made it obvious I wasn't enjoying watching hers (an old MGM musical). We both checked the time frequently.

By early afternoon I'd retreated to my room and my drawing. An hour later she knocked on the door. When I didn't answer, she pounded.

"Enter, please," I said primly.

I looked up from the easel as the door swung open. She glanced around. What did she expect to see—a naked fourteen-year-old boy? "I'm alone," I said.

She cocked her head and pursed her lips. I counted, One, two, three—yes, there was the sigh. Oh, Mom. So predictable, you had to love her. I set down my pencil. "This has been a lousy day."

She smiled. "Yes." She came in and sat on my bed. "Would you mind terribly if I went out with Charles?"

"No."

"There's a meet-the-baby thing at his daughter and son-in-law's house."

"Why didn't you say so earlier?"

"Because it's Sunday and I didn't plan on going. But the way things have been today, I thought why not. You're invited too, by the way."

"Uh-uh." I picked up the pencil and shaded Will's beard a bit. "Is the ex-wife going to be there?"

"Both of them. Jenna's very close to her stepmother. Ex-stepmother."

I whistled. "A party with both of his exes? That's a big step, Mom. Is it one you want to take?"

She nodded. "I think I do." She rose and walked over to look at the drawing. I closed my eyes and tried to guess her reaction by the vibes.

No go. She's too good an actress.

Finally, hands landed on my shoulders and massaged. "You are so gifted, it sometimes frightens me. Aerin was—"

"Is," I said sharply. "She's alive."

"True, especially in this drawing. I love how you've staged the scene: What just happened, that's what I want to know. What did Aerin say to make everyone laugh? How intriguing. No, dear, what I was going to say about her is that she, too, was a prodigiously gifted young woman."

"She still is. She's only twenty-two."

"You're right; that's very young. I wonder if she feels young. You've made Aerin and her mother look so much alike. Do they? I don't recall. Well, that's a stupid question—why else would you have done it that way."

"We don't look alike, do we?"

"Not so much, I suppose. But sometimes as the child gets older a resemblance gets clearer."

"Then do you suppose you look like your mother?"

The hands stopped massaging. "I haven't ever thought about it," she said coolly.

"Never? I find that hard to believe. Do you think that maybe I look like her?"

"Hard to say, Hanna. I have no memories of her and there are only those few pictures. You've seen them, you know where they are; feel free to look and decide for yourself."

"But don't you ever wonder how the hell I got to be five ten? That's taller than Grandpa and taller than Dad was, right?"

"Yes."

I swiveled the chair around until we were facing each other. "What would have happened to me if you had died after Dad did? Don't tell me Grandpa would've taken over. I can't believe he would've agreed to raise another girl."

"Ray and Julia."

"You're kidding."

"Not at all. We were very close. Still are."

"It shouldn't surprise me, I guess. I mean, considering our family, there weren't many options."

"Considering our friends, there were quite a few." She

turned back to the drawing. "A happy family in a sunny kitchen," she said. "I hope you—" She held back the words by chewing on her lip.

I tilted back my chair. "Hope what?" The sharp edge to my voice surprised even me.

Her gaze shifted from the desk to me. "It's not surprising that you'd wonder about . . . things, especially about my mother." Her voice had again cooled. "I wish I knew more to tell you." She acknowledged the discarded sketches strewn about with a flip of her hand. "All these drawings of the Walkers. I hope you aren't suddenly unhappy with your life because you've fallen in love with another family." She kissed the top of my head. "We're a happy family, Hanna. Please don't forget that."

She was halfway down the stairs before I caught up. "Mom, say hi to Charles and Jenna and Josh and hug their baby for me and tell me it's really okay if I don't go."

"It's really okay. And I'm grateful that you don't mind if I do go."

"It shouldn't be that big a deal, really. Maybe it's time we rethink Sundays, anyway. It's all going to change soon enough when I leave for school."

"Hanna, what's wrong?"

I'd sat down, though I landed so hard and ungracefully, I suppose she thought I'd fallen. There was a dust bunny in the corner of a step. I blew. It rose and hung in the air for a second before falling. "I was supposed to vacuum, wasn't I? Sorry."

"Hanna, please."

Ah, those worried blues. "Mom, I think I'm about to have a fight with Maura or Kelsey, maybe even both of them. A serious fight. One that matters."

"Don't."

"It's not that simple. I don't know how I can say what I have to say to them without it happening. I'm so mad about something."

"What's going on?"

I spotted another clump of dust on the landing. Mom was so orderly, how did she put up with me? "What would you consider a serious betrayal?"

She sat on the step below me. "Infidelity." She watched for a reaction. "Divulging a confidence." When my eyes skitted away, she made a soft noise, no doubt giving herself points for the direct hit. "Hanna—"

I shook my head fiercely. She rose and went down the stairs. She came back shortly with our coats. I wiped my cheeks with my palms. "Mom, please, no. I don't want to go to a party."

She held out my parka. "Put it on. And that's not what we're doing." She jiggled the coat.

I walked down and took the coat. "I'd love to get out. But where?"

She smoothed my hair. "The art institute is open for another hour. It's been months since you showed me your current favorite paintings."

I checked my pockets for a tissue—even a used one would do. She held out a fresh one. I blew my nose. "Still the Corot and the Manet. Nothing's changed." Our eyes met as the words registered.

Everything had changed.

→←

After the museum and a light supper at our favorite café I dropped her off to catch the end of the party. I went home and made the grandparent calls. I almost got the nerve to ask my grandfather something about Mom's mom, but his wife was on the line too and she was so cheery, I didn't have the heart to dampen the mood.

Those were the easy calls.

><

I'd thought about it all night after the party and through most of the day and kept coming up with the same answer: What's the point of a friendship if you can't trust the friend?

Maura didn't see it that way. "Hanna, don't be so melodramatic." She batted the salt shaker between her palms until it finally tipped and fell on the table.

Kelsey said nothing. For the longest time she'd been staring past my shoulder, either to avoid eye contact or because she'd spotted something or someone more interesting. Which I doubted.

Okay, I thought. Her silence was one big fat clue. Obviously Kelsey had talked to Zak and he had talked to the world. She briefly met my gaze.

A waitress came by with coffee. "Want me to leave the whole pot?" she said as she refilled cups.

"Sure," said Maura.

"No," I said. I didn't plan on staying much longer.

"Whatever," the waitress replied, leaving it on the table.

Kelsey passed me the creamer. "Did it occur to you, Hanna, that maybe that boy talked?"

"His name is Will. And it never occurred to me. He wouldn't."

"You dumped him, so maybe he was getting back at you."

"You don't understand, he— " He had something to hide too, but I couldn't say that. "He just wouldn't."

"But right away you assumed your oldest friends would." Kelsey's tone was razor sharp and very angry.

"Oh, for god's sake, you two," Maura said. "I told Brian, okay?"

Kelsey and I stared at her.

"I am incredibly sorry, Hanna. But like I said, you are going way overboard. And I'm not sure you're being fair, expecting us to not tell our boyfriends something so huge."

"Something so huge is exactly what I expect you to keep quiet. What if it gets back to him? What if some distorted version of what I told you about Aerin shows up in some magazine?"

"I said I'm sorry," Maura pleaded.

"What else have you told him?" Kelsey asked, her voice still sharp and angry.

They faced off. Finally Maura said, "Nothing." She waited, watching Kelsey. "I mean it."

Holy crap. Obviously there was something they shared that I didn't know.

Maura slumped into the corner of the booth. "Okay, this is what happened: Brian and I got wasted Friday night. We'd done a wild improv show and I just felt like going crazy. We smoked way too much weed, and then he started getting after me about why I won't sleep with him. Before I knew it I guess I was babying him and proving he meant something to me by telling him Hanna's juicy secret. Obviously the jackass thought it was too good to keep to himself. He's going to hear about it, I can tell you. It might be the last conversation I ever have with him. Hanna, I would not hurt you for anything in the world and I'm truly, deeply sorry. But don't go on a power thing and make me keep saying it."

I rose and put enough money on the table to cover the whole bill. "I won't. I don't need to hear it ever again."

⇥⇤

Monday morning I didn't show up in the kitchen until Mom had her coat on and was shaking the car keys impatiently.

She shook her head when I shuffled in sleepily, still in pajamas. I stood in front of the coffeepot. She'd left one cup. It smelled so good, but could I go back to sleep if I had some?

"Don't you feel well?" she asked.

"You know, I don't even remember when I started drinking coffee. And now I have a horrible habit. What are the chances of getting a mental health day? Would you mind calling me in sick? I promise I won't waste the day. I'll sleep some more, get up and study, then go to Whipple and work on the set with Tom." I faced her. "Last night I found out that Maura told Brian something I asked her not to tell and now it's all over the school and beyond. And I don't think I ever want to see her again. Do you suppose Tom painted the stage over the weekend? I'm having second thoughts about the black we chose."

Mom put her hands on my shoulders, studied me, then said, "I'll make the call."

⇥⇤

I got away with it for two days. On Wednesday she pounded on my door and shouted, "Get out of bed; you're going to school."

She dropped me off and watched until I was inside. I waved from behind the glass door. She waved back, but still didn't drive away. Fine. I had business to take care of and I didn't plan on ditching.

The counseling office was already crowded. A lot of the kids waiting were seniors, every single one apparently in panic mode about college apps or test scores. I pretended interest in a college brochure until the secretary called my name. She gave me an exasperated look even before I opened my mouth. "Hanna, please don't tell me that suddenly you want to apply to more schools than the one in Rhode Island and now you need transcripts sent out ASAP. We discussed this in the fall and I begged you then to apply to more than one place."

That's one thing I love about this big old institution: Over two thousand kids in the school and the secretaries still know your face and case. "That's not it, Mrs. Delaney. I need to see my counselor."

"Cynthia's first opening is tomorrow at three. If it's a transcript request form you need, they're on the counter."

"I don't want a transcript. I want to drop out. Are there forms for that?"

Miraculously, my counselor was suddenly free.

I swung my bag onto one of the chairs in her office and sat in another. Before she could even greet me or find my file in the computer, I was talking. "I'm serious about this, Miss Roberts. I've had enough. No arguing. Count my credits and tell me I can forget second semester."

She studied the file as it opened on the screen. She inhaled deeply, swiveled her chair, and faced me as she folded her hands on the desk. Exhaled. "Hanna, it's not unusual—"

I held up a hand. "No lectures. Just a credit count."

"But you're registered for Don Laney's senior drawing seminar next term."

"Not what I asked."

"Yes, Hanna, once you complete this current semester, you have the credits you need to graduate. We'd need your parents to sign—"

"I'm eighteen. I'll sign what's necessary. And it's parent, singular. My father's dead."

She glued her gaze to the computer. "That's right; sorry. And eighteen may be good enough for buying cigarettes and voting, but it doesn't make you an adult inside these walls. We need a Consent to Leave form signed by a parent or guardian." She swiveled her chair again, opened a file drawer, and pulled out a paper. "Would you still want to walk with your class at graduation?"

"Let's make that a maybe."

"Well, then, once you bring this back with your mother's signature, all you need to worry about is getting through your finals next week." When I didn't say anything, she smiled. "You're stunned I don't try to talk you out of it. Don't be. I've got eleven students to see before lunch. Three are facing deportation and the others are in serious academic or legal trouble. A case of senioritis is nothing. You've done the work here, you're not involved in any extracurricular activities, so why hang around? I can't say I blame you, Hanna."

→‹

I spent the rest of the day in negotiations and won them all. They were dark victories, though: While I'd talked my way out of every one of my finals, I'd be writing five ten-page papers.

I avoided the cafeteria. This was partly by design and partly because I'd needed the extra time to persuade my aquatic biology teacher to agree to the paper-for-exam exchange. So it was after school by the time Kelsey caught up with me.

Good old Kelsey—she went straight to the point. "You and Maura have put me in a really tough spot."

"I know. Sorry. And I'm sorry I didn't return your calls. I've been thinking things over." I carried an armload of papers and notebooks to the trash can and dumped them.

She leaned against the lockers. "I figured that much. Hanna, what she did was inexcusable, but for the sake of the friendship you could cut her some slack. At least don't do the silent thing you're so good at. Talk to me. Yell at her."

I turned, picked up the stack of coloring books and the box of crayons, and walked across the hall. Melissa, one of the regulars at Hanna's Table, was pulling her coat out of a locker. "I bequeath these to you," I said cheerfully. "You're in charge of the table now."

She looked stunned as she took them. "Why?"

"I'll be gone for a while," I said as I walked away. No sense in going into it with a freshman. I crouched down and put the rest of the junk from my locker into my bag.

Kelsey had heard me. "What do you mean?" she said, suspicion shading her voice. "Where are you going?"

I closed my locker for the very last time. "Whipple. I've got to start painting the backdrop."

She laid a hand on my arm. "Hanna, cut it out."

I faced her. "I'm done here. I've got enough credits to skip next term. I don't have any finals, so I'm out the door today."

"You're quitting school just because you're mad at us? Maura's right—you're really overreacting."

"You think so? Maybe that's because she kept your secret—whatever it is—and blabbered mine. I don't want to get in a fight with you, Kels. This isn't about us. But if you keep on taking her side and ganging up on me and telling me I'm overreacting, it might be."

I got about five steps down the hall. She practically barked my name. "Hanna!"

I turned around.

She walked forward slowly. "That secret of mine? You may as well know, it's about Spence and me. We've been e-mailing and talking and I just don't know where it's going. That's why I asked her to keep something from you. We're not ganging up on you. I just don't know where it's going yet with him, and there's Zak to figure out." She finally dared a look at my face. She sagged.

"Spence and you? Kelsey, you know he's nothing to me—wait, that sounds so insulting. He's a great guy and, wow, now that I see it, you two are a perfect match, in the best way."

She didn't look cheered.

I rubbed her arm. "Who made the first move? I knew he'd get over me fast. I think this is terrific. Tricky about Zak, of course. He's sweet too."

Maybe it was how she avoided looking at me. Or the way she looked so weak, leaning against the locker. Or maybe it was just a gut guess. "Oh my god," I said, stepping back. "It started before I dumped him." I waited for her denial. Silence. "He made such a fuss when I did it. What a liar."

"He's not," she said sharply. "He really was upset because he really liked you. He felt awful about what we did." She swore under her breath and bit her lip.

I put a hand on her shoulder and turned her so I could see her expression. "What you *did*?"

She wouldn't lift her eyes; even so, her face revealed everything: confirmation, guilt, misery.

"You hooked up with my boyfriend when he and I were still going out?"

"No! It didn't go anywhere beyond some stupid drunken . . . kisses."

"Only kisses? How absolutely admirable, considering he was your best friend's boyfriend. When did this drunken groping happen?"

"Thanksgiving. You and your mom were in New York and Zak was at his uncle's. Spence and I ran into each other at a party near the U. Neither of us knew many people there, so we sort of hung out."

"Hung out? That's one way to put it, I suppose."

"C'mon, Hanna, you of all people should understand that it's pretty damn easy to let things slide out of control. It was one stupid night."

"Except that you've been e-mailing and talking ever since. Talking plenty about me, I bet. Does Zak know?"

She shook her head. "Just Maura."

I recalled Spencer's stunned look when I told him that I wanted to break up and his certainty it was because of something Maura had said. "Now I get it," I murmured. "It wasn't me he was calling a bitch."

"He knew I'd told Maura. He was convinced she told you. Hanna, it happened once. We were totally out of it, and that's the only reason anything happened and I'm sorry."

I put a hand on her shoulder and pulled until she faced me. "Those roses . . . You were so surprised to hear he'd never given me any. I bet you got some."

"Once," she whispered. "The day after . . ."

"You mean the day after you almost had sex with him."

"They came with a note that said he thought it was all a mistake and that you meant too much to him."

"Sweet, but I think I'd care more if *you* had sent the note to *him*."

She stiffened. "Maura and I both screwed up, Hanna, but please don't make it worse than it has to be. Let's take care of this. I've got to go to practice now, but let's get together tonight and fix things."

"Fix things? What the hell can be fixed?"

"Don't, Hanna," she shouted as I walked away. "Don't turn your back and run off."

Fix things, fix things, fix things. I raised an arm and slashed the air. Fix you.

I'd nearly reached the end of the hall before I looked back. She was frozen in place, arms crossed over her physics text.

I pushed open the door, shuddered at the blast of cold air, and left school.

5
Aerin

When you break up with a boyfriend you can always talk to your friends, but who do you talk to when you dump your friends? Mom would have loved it if I'd unloaded on her, but I didn't want her to know everything. We've always been careful about not confiding too much in each other. It's intense enough living side by side, and if I made her my primary spill site, there's no telling—

"Hanna, you've hardly talked since we sat down at the table."

I tossed back the remaining drops of the single glass of wine she always allowed me if we'd cooked a worthy meal. I reached for the wine bottle. Everything was upside down, why not bend all the rules?

Her hand covered mine on the bottle's neck and pushed it back down on the table. "Since you don't feel like talking, I'll tell you about my day. Kelsey called me at school this afternoon." She served herself a second helping of salad.

I looked over the table at the elaborate dinner she'd

cooked after a long work day. "That explains all this. Did you two have a nice talk?"

"She's very upset that you've all had this fight."

"So am I, Mom. But a big part of 'this fight' has to do with trusting and not talking, and so I, for one, am not going to say any more. It's between Maura and Kelsey and me."

I left the table and came back with a pen and the school's consent form. "While Kelsey was crying on your shoulder, I bet she told you about this too. Don't waste your breath trying to talk me out of it. But since I know you will, please remember that I have enough credits to graduate. I don't need to be there. I'll do the ceremony in June if you want me to."

Well, blow me away. She scanned the paper, signed, and handed it back.

"Kelsey did mention it, and I'm grateful, as it gave me time to think it over." She refilled her wineglass and then poured me a miserly second serving. "Sometimes school is the wrong place to be," she said. "Don't quote me on that, especially to anyone you might run into at Whipple. I'd probably get fired. I suspect you could use your time more wisely than warming chairs at Humphrey next semester. Do you have a plan? I won't tolerate moping twenty-four-seven, but I expect you know that."

I stared at her signature on the form. Back in seventh grade I'd spent hours trying unsuccessfully to copy it. "I'll work more shifts at the store and save some money."

"Good. Anything else?"

I shrugged.

"You could be more involved with the spring show, you

know. Tom and I would both love that. We're doing *Anything Goes* and—" I must have made a face, because hers suddenly darkened. "Well then, maybe you should take an art class."

"Mom, this has all blown up so fast that I haven't had a chance to get things straight, but if you leave me alone I'll figure it out, okay?"

"Fine. I won't push. But, Hanna, you have this sudden gift of extra time. Why not use it to immerse yourself in what you love?" Her eyes softened in focus. "That's what I told the Walkers."

"Now you've lost me."

"The day Aerin left Whipple I told her parents that school can be the wrong place to be for some children, and that I certainly thought that was the case for her, even though she was only fourteen."

"I can't believe you actually told Whipple parents not to bother with school."

"They weren't Whipple parents at that point. Aerin had just been expelled, and they'd come to pick her up and get what most certainly was a lecture from the dean. I chased them down before they left and we talked in the parking lot." She picked the remaining olive out of the salad bowl and popped it into her mouth. "I can still see her watching us from their car—just a terrified young girl."

"She told me that she didn't ever hit you like it got reported. I always thought she had. Until I actually met her, it was sort of a cool thing: My mom got slugged by a future rock star."

She made a face. "All part of the myth of Aerin Walker. She tried, but I got out of the way. It happened during an exercise in beginning acting class. I can't even recall exactly how it happened. She was always so wound up. Oh, but her musical ability was astounding. Sometimes she'd play piano before class and improvise and mesmerize everyone."

"So after she got kicked out for attacking you—"

Mom held up a hand. "That wasn't the only reason. There were other infractions that didn't involve me, and I don't remember what they were."

"I won't ask, don't worry. I still find it hard to believe that you'd advise parents to forget about school for a kid."

"Not that kid. She'd been in a number of schools over the years. Mark Walker's well known as a public education advocate, so it was rather a surprise when one of his children enrolled at Whipple. I imagine he and his wife hoped the tough academics would be the right challenge for her. Like so many troubled students, she tested off the charts. I did not lecture them, but I did say that I thought they shouldn't bother trying to find another school, even an arts school. I had no doubt that she'd fail at the next place."

"What an awful thing to tell someone's parents."

She shrugged. "Doesn't help to lie. I suggested that they pretend to homeschool her to satisfy the district while they immersed her in music and bought her all the lessons and tutors they could afford. I gather they took my advice. I think I remember reading somewhere that she hasn't been in school since Whipple." Mom finished her wine. Her eyes were bright and wet. "Is she terribly sad, Hanna?"

"I think so. And why shouldn't she be? She's lived

through a nightmare: She was driving the car when her friends died."

Her eyes suddenly cleared and she took a deep breath. Before she could blurt out something about me losing *my* friends, I rose and started clearing dishes. "Thanks for understanding about school, Mom." I kissed the top of her head. "And you were right the other night: We are a happy family."

><

As soon as word spread that I wasn't returning to Humphrey, I got plenty of phone calls and e-mails. People were sweet and envious. We made promises back and forth about keeping in touch, which at first seemed absurd because, come on—I wasn't moving to Thailand. But then, only a week after I walked out the school door, someone slipped up in an IM and mentioned that there'd been a party I'd known nothing about. Of course, it was at Joe's and he's tight with Zak, so it made sense that I wasn't invited. I wouldn't have gone, anyway. But the way absolutely no one talked about it with me—am I paranoid, or does that stink conspiracy?

Two days after the party I got an e-mail from Cate: *Would someone please explain what's going on? First you and Spence break up, then Maura dumps Brian, and as of last night Kels and Zak are finished. And NO ONE is talking about any of it. Are you guys jinxed or something?*

Jinxed is a good word for it, I replied. *Better keep your distance.*

After that I blew off most of the other e-mails and phone calls, dealing with people's curiosity either with a glib evasion or by ignoring them entirely. After another week the phone never rang and e-mails were down to zero and the few times I signed on to IM, no one was ever online. Had everyone blocked me? Easy enough to find out, by creating a new IM identity, but I decided not to bother. I decided not to care.

Still, I wondered: How had I become the bad guy?

My manager, though, was thrilled about the changes in my life. As soon as I e-mailed my final papers to the teachers, I gave her the green light to add hours to my schedule. I became a working girl.

The first Friday night I got home after a thirty-hour week at the store, I was dead. As I fumbled for my keys, I heard voices and soft piano music coming from inside the house. Charles was in Canada for a couple of weeks doing a guest professor thing at some law school, so it was probably Mom's friends making the noise. I leaned against the door for a moment, almost too weary to go in and be cheerful.

Aerin Walker was at the piano. She pounded a couple of loud chords as I entered the living room. "I just dropped in unannounced," she said. "How rude is that? Caught your mom in her pajamas."

Mom was curled up on the couch. I unbuttoned my coat and flopped down next to her. "Aerin's been improvising something for the show," she said. "Thornton Wilder might roll over in his grave, but I think there are a number of places that could use a bit of incidental music, especially the start of the second act. She came up with something right away. Aerin, would you please play that piece again?"

When Aerin had finished, she turned around. "You don't like it. I can tell by the expression."

When I didn't answer, Mom said, "She does like it; she's just thinking about something else."

"I'm thinking," I said slowly, "that if you use it, which I think you should, we might have to change the way the chairs are placed."

Mom nodded. "I see it as almost a ballet now, and the cast should enter . . ."

She and I tossed ideas back and forth. Aerin listened for a bit, then resumed playing softly.

Finally Mom rose with a satisfied sigh. "I'm meeting friends for breakfast and I should get to bed. I'll never be able to sleep, but I should at least try." She hugged Aerin and then stood back to study her. A smile crept out. "My, but you look like your brother."

"I don't think we're supposed to mention him," Aerin said.

I stood. "I'm getting a snack."

Aerin followed me into the kitchen. "Heard about school," she said. "Congrats, I guess."

I opened the fridge. "Thanks. Want something to eat? I think I'll have Cheerios."

She laughed. "Will has a bowl of cereal every night before he goes to bed."

"We're not supposed to mention him." I shut the fridge door. "I don't want to seem unfriendly, but I'm surprised to see you."

She shrugged and leaned against the counter. "After that day you came to our house, I got to thinking about your mother. I was browsing for CDs in Uptown tonight. I caught the bus to go to my grandparents', but then I had the inspiration to get off and stop in here."

"How did you know where we live? We're not in the phone book."

"Will showed me the other night. He and Beth and I were headed home from Grandma's. We made a slight detour because he wanted to point out your house. He also made us stop at the lake so he could show us the spot where he found her. It's so strange how people have the impulse to make those memorials." She retreated into her head for a moment. "There was a huge one by the highway after the accident. Or so I heard. I've never been on that road since. I should go."

I touched her arm lightly. "Sure about the Cheerios?"

She smiled. "I'll wait and have some with Will. It'll be fun to tell him that's what you offered. Oh, maybe I won't. He's pretty heartbroken as it is and knowing he's lost a girl who likes cereal for a bedtime snack would just about destroy him. Yeah, I know: Cork it, Aerin."

It was another cold snowy night, and when I offered to drive her to her grandparents', she accepted gratefully. Except for her occasional directions, we didn't talk during the short trip, mostly because she was humming and singing softly and because I was concentrating on the icy streets as I tuned in to my private Aerin Walker concert.

I double-parked in front of her grandparents' house, a large brick two-story a block from one of the lakes. Every window was illuminated. "Bright enough to be a lighthouse," I said.

"Perfect metaphor," said Aerin. "That's pretty much what it is to me. Always brings me in for a safe landing."

I drummed a rhythm on my leg. "Not to get too analytical, but I'd guess it's not so perfect as a metaphor. After all, aren't lighthouses always built on the dangerous spots?"

Aerin laughed. "Well, Hanna, families are like that, right?"

"I guess. I don't really have much—" Her cell trilled shrilly, and she swore as she twisted to dig into a pocket and turn it off. "Take the call," I said.

She gestured toward her grandparents'. "It's probably just someone in there wondering where I am. What were you going to say?"

"Nothing," I said softly as I watched the house. A young girl twirled through the well-lit space behind a big window; several people milled about behind her. "Looks like a party."

"Just family. It's sort of Grand Central for all the cousins and everyone."

"That must be nice."

"Want to come in?" Aerin said. "I know Will would be glad to see you."

"Are you nuts?"

She laughed. "Grandma was a psych nurse for a long time. She says 'nuts' is not a clinical term and she hates it when her grandchildren use it, which we do quite a lot, usually when we talk to each other. 'Crazy' is her other least favorite label. Okay, Hanna, be shy. Some other time, maybe."

I shook my head. No other time. "My grandmother . . ."
She waited.

"My grandmother lives in Florida. We're not very close." I shifted and faced her. "You're lucky."

She was silhouetted by the frail beam of a streetlamp, but I could detect a smile. "It's been a long time since anyone has called me lucky," Aerin said. She opened the door, but didn't move from her seat. The pale beam of the dome light illuminated little more than her face. She had two short parallel scars near her left temple and one running along her chin. I wondered if they were from the accident. I worked hard to not look at her wrists. If the magazines had gotten it right, there should be some there as well, the result of a suicide attempt a few hours after the accident.

I bit my lip. Lucky—I'd actually said *that* to Aerin Walker?

She cleared her throat. "So you're feeling a bit of guilt about those kids who died."

I faced forward and gripped the steering wheel. "Will's talked, I guess."

"What can I say—the boy's heartbroken. He spilled his guts. Don't panic. He told the family about you talking with those kids that night, but the rest was just to me." She closed the car door and the light went off. "Funny thing, guilt. No matter what anyone says and no matter the reality of what happened, it's hard to shake. On the good days it's like a low noise that won't go away. Bad days . . ." She hummed a bit, shaking her head slowly. "Having dreams about it?"

"Off and on. Mostly the same one: dark water and their faces."

"That would keep you from sleeping." She whistled a few notes. "For the longest time after the accident I couldn't look at a window at night without seeing their faces looking in."

"You lost so much so fast." Shit. Rip your tongue out, Hanna. Why had I said that?

"Yes."

"How did you make it stop—god, listen to me. It's not as if me talking to those kids before their accident even remotely compares to—"

Aerin's hand shot out and her index finger pressed against my lips. "Hush; it's not a competition." Her hand dropped. "Now what were you going to say about making something stop?"

"How did you stop everything from spinning out of control?"

She stretched out her arm and tugged up the coat sleeve, revealing a pale line on a slender wrist. "I didn't." Her arm fell.

"That happened just after the accident, right?"

"It didn't 'happen,' Hanna; I cut my wrists. I tried to kill myself. My friends were dead and I wanted to die too."

"I can't believe I'm making you talk about this. I didn't mean to do that, Aerin."

She crossed her arms. "I know. You wanted to talk about those kids and the thing with my brother and how everything's suddenly upside down and you don't know what the hell is going on. Hanna, when I feel things are spinning out of control I tend to barricade myself where I feel safe. Home or over here, usually. And when it gets really tough I head to Tucson."

"You hide or run away." I bit my lip again. Would someone please tape my mouth shut?

"I suppose it looks like that, but since I always have my memories and messed-up head with me, I don't think I'm really getting away from anything."

"Why Tucson?"

She shivered. "It's warmer. I stay with friends who've known me since day one. They have a winter place with a guesthouse that they've pretty much let me take over. It has a piano. I keep a guitar there. They leave me alone but are always ready if I want to talk. Mom or Grandma or Beth usually shows up and everybody takes turns keeping an eye on me because no matter what I tell them, they're all scared that I'll hurt myself again. It's not like I'm chained to guards, though; I have room to breathe. Some days I walk in the desert. Some days I just stare at the piano. Sometimes I even play. I guess that sounds pretty screwed up, but . . ." She reached for the heater control on the dash and turned it up. "I didn't play a thing for over a year after the crash. Then one day I just had to. You must know how that is. You draw and paint, I play and sing—that's how we deal with what's rolling around in our brains. It's easier not to fight it. Do what you do and just try to make it mean something."

"Like potato chip jingles?" I made a face. Not again.

Aerin laughed. "You can't help yourself, can you? I like that. Okay, sometimes what's rolling around in the head is crap, but you've got to work that out too. I guess . . ." She clenched her hands. She murmured something to herself.

Be patient. Be silent.

She suddenly leaned over and pointed out the window. "North Star. Amazing, isn't it, how even in the city you can spot it? Sometimes, Hanna, you're so far out there's no lighthouse, but the star is always there. Ever think about what it must have been like for explorers way back when? One tiny, true point in the sky, and that's all they needed to make it across dark crazy water." She pulled back. "Are you free tomorrow night, by any chance? There's this band I've heard good things about. Beth usually goes with me when I get the itch to hear music, but she's got a date."

I must have had some weird expression on my face, because she laughed. "Are you shocked because my sister has a date or because I asked you to hang out?"

No, I thought. Just catching my breath from the U-turn in mood. Obviously we'd gone to the edge of something and she'd needed to pull back. "I don't know Beth well enough to be shocked about her date. It's the invitation."

"The thing is, I need a ride. I won't drive anymore and the place is over in Wisconsin. The other thing is, I know you don't freak out about being with me, and you obviously know how to keep your mouth shut and not blab to the world about meeting the tragic Aerin Walker. I appreciate that, Hanna."

But I hadn't kept my mouth shut. Guilt and anger roiled.

"Never mind," she said softly. "It was just a thought."

"It sounds like fun, Aerin," I said quickly, "and I'm flattered, but I'm not such great company these days. I only seem to . . . cause trouble."

Aerin laughed again. "Well, according to you I'm lucky, so that balances things out. C'mon, if the band's any good it could be fun. If it's not we can at least wallow together, though lately I've been feeling a little maxed out on self-pity. Can you get the car?"

"Probably."

"Good." She spotted a gas receipt and a pen in the slot under the CD player. She pulled them out and handed them to me. "Give me your e-mail or phone. We'll connect tomorrow to set up a time."

I shook the pen a few times to get the cold ink flowing. "I should warn you about something else."

"I can't even imagine what it could be."

"I may not look like my mother, but under special circumstances it's obvious that I'm her daughter." I handed her the receipt and she tucked it into a pocket.

"You say that like it's a bad thing."

"You could regret inviting me, that's all. If the band's halfway decent, it will be hard to get me off the dance floor."

>←

The dark stillness in my house was like a sick joke after seeing the cheery scene at Aerin's grandparents'.

"I will not wallow," I announced to the empty kitchen. "I have maxed out on self-pity."

The screen saver's glow was the only light in my room. Mona Lisa ricocheted across the monitor. I jiggled the mouse to bring up the desktop. A gaudy banner pulsed: *2 new messages*. No human I know can resist that. I brought up my e-mail and scanned the senders' names: ImprovQueen—Maura—and WalkerTwo. Aerin?

I opened up WalkerTwo's message.

Hanna: Thanks for the lift tonight. Hope you're not feeling guilty about the conversation because it's good for me to talk. Tomorrow should be fun, glad you're willing. As soon as I got inside I was reminded by several people that I'd promised to show up at one of Dad's political things tomor-

row. *We all take turns being supportive and now it's my turn. Could you pick me up at the Machinists' Union Hall (Colby and 26th) at 7:30 instead of at my house? If you aren't there by eight I'll figure you can't make it. Don't worry, you won't run into Will. BTW, he's downstairs playing poker with Grandma and losing badly.*

AW

PS: Don't wallow.

I sent a quick reply that didn't mention Will. Then I opened Maura's message.

H: K & I would love to talk whenever you're ready. Miss you. M.

My hand hovered over the keyboard a few seconds, then a finger landed on "Delete."

Don't wallow. Well, I wouldn't.

Cheerful me quickly composed and sent identical messages to each of my grandparents: *Cold and snowy here. Hope you're well. Love, Hanna.*

Cheerful me hummed as I got ready for bed. Cheerful me drew an elaborate, whimsical border on the note I scribbled and taped to the fridge: *Need the car Sat. nite. Okay?*

But it was wallowing me by the time I returned to my room and sat at the computer. I pulled Maura's message out of the "Deleted" folder and read it again. As I did I heard Aerin: *You obviously know how to keep your mouth shut.* I stilled the anger with a few short breaths and then dumped Maura's e-mail for good.

Wallowing me pulled out a sketch pad and hastily drew several half-assed pictures of a glowing, storybook brick house.

And it was definitely wallowing me who went to the spare bedroom that Mom used as an office and pulled open the deep drawer in her desk. I reached up and flicked on a lamp as I searched through the hanging files.

Cortland, Lydia had been pulled out of order and put in the back. Had Mom tired of seeing it every time she flipped through the files? The folder held two envelopes. One had the name and address of an Atlanta law firm printed in the corner; the other was thin, blue, and unmarked.

Back in my room, I opened the blue envelope and pulled out three black-and-white photos. *Grandmother* was never a term that seemed right the rare times I thought about my mother's mother. It was especially wrong for the young woman in these pictures. "Lydia," I whispered, picking one up, "you were a beautiful girl." A tall beautiful girl. She and my grandfather stood ankle deep in the water at a beach, their arms linked and their eyes glued on each other.

I turned it over. Feminine handwriting in faded blue ink: *Honeymoon, Key West, my 20th birthday. Catching our breath!*

What happened next? I thought, turning it back over and looking again at the amorous couple.

Well, okay, I could probably guess what happened next.

The second photo showed a glamorous Lydia in a sleek evening gown leaning forward and happily accepting a light for her cigarette from a man in a tux. One of her breasts threatened to spill out of the deep neckline of the dress. Grandpa and a woman stood in the background, both of them watching with sour expressions.

On the back in blue: *BP New Year's party, 1952, Caracas. Shame on me!*

My mother had been born in Venezuela, where Grandpa worked for British Petroleum prospecting drilling sites. Lydia had left for good while they were still living there.

Yes, shame on you, I thought, studying the picture again. And what happened next?

The last picture was a family photo. Grandpa was dressed for field work. My mother stood by her mother's side, clutching her skirt and looking up at her with a familiar intense expression. Lydia's face was vacant and dull.

Claudia's 3rd birthday. Sam departs again.

I flipped back to the picture. What happened next?

That much I knew: She walked away.

I placed the photos in a row, wondering why there were just the three. I picked up the party scene picture and held it under the light. There were faint brown spots on the scalloped edging of the photo paper. Scorch marks? In the albums and frames downstairs there were quite a few pictures of Mom as a baby and toddler, but she was alone or with just Grandpa in all of those. Had there been a moment of pain and rage when he'd gathered and set a match to the ones with Lydia, then changed his mind and salvaged these three?

"What happened?" I whispered.

The envelope from the law firm was postmarked forty years ago and was addressed to Dr. Samuel Tucker. Grandpa. I lifted the flap and pulled out a heavy sheet of paper. I unfolded it, smoothing the creases under my thumb. Mom had never shown me this. No wonder.

At the request of our clients, Peter and Carolyn Cortland, we are informing you that they have moved and do not wish to disclose the new address. In the event communication with the Cortland family is absolutely necessary, please contact this office.

Absolutely necessary—like when someone died?

I swiveled my chair back to the computer.

According to the Internet, the Atlanta law firm of Faber, Hooten, and Stoll was now Faber, Hooten, Stoll, Deaver, and Krall. According to the obituary archive of the *Atlanta Constitution,* Peter Cortland died four years ago, his wife, Carolyn, a year later. According to her death notice she was survived only by one daughter, Lydia Cortland of Barcelona, Spain.

Spain?

I Googled "Lydia Cortland" and came up with nothing more than another version of her mother's obituary. "You're very good at vanishing," I murmured. "But I'm going to find you."

I started and restarted a letter seven times before ripping all the attempts into shreds and sweeping them off the desk into the trash. I rocked the desk chair slightly and stared at the wall before pulling down one of the pastel drawings Will had admired. I scribbled a message on the back and slipped it into an envelope.

>‹

The entrance to the union hall was tucked between a Korean video store and a nail salon. Smokers formed a gauntlet on the sidewalk. The group seemed to be evenly split between men and women; the coat of choice split between bowling jackets and army-green parkas. I dipped my head in greeting whenever I caught someone eyeing me.

Was everyone a machinist? Were there no machinists under the age of sixty?

A sign was taped to an interior wall of the union lobby: "Local 2291 welcomes postal retirees and friends. Dinner with Congressman Walker, 2nd floor."

The lobby was furnished sparely: one bench and an artificial ficus tree. One of the branches of the ficus had snapped and it drooped nearly to the floor. A green arrow pointing up blinked above the open door of an elevator.

The elevator opened onto a similar lobby on the second floor. This one had two benches and a healthier fake plant. A loud mix of voices rolled out of an open wide doorway.

The meeting room was packed, but it looked like the dinner was over. People stood in small groups and pairs. Mr. Walker was at the center of one of the larger clusters, listening intently to an angry man.

I stepped into a corner near an overloaded coatrack and scanned the crowd for Aerin. A public meeting seemed like an odd place for a total recluse to hang out. Of course, "total recluse" had been Maura's term and she got it from *Rolling Stone,* which had been wrong about Aerin punching Mom, so maybe—

"What are you doing here?"

Will's accusing voice pierced through the din. He stood a few feet away, just inside the doorway I'd entered. He had a gym bag over his shoulder. He slung it toward the coatrack. It hit the wall and dropped to the floor.

I raised my hand. "Hey," I said weakly and walked over to him. "I'm meeting Aerin."

That puzzled him. He narrowed his eyes, unzipped his jacket, slid his hands into the back pockets of his jeans, and slumped into basic Will Walker posture. "I just called home to find a ride. Mom said Aerin was going out with Beth tonight."

"She's going out with me. Beth has a date."

He looked around, then pointed. Beth was shaking hands with people near the front of the room. She saw us and waved.

"Well, maybe she's meeting him later," I said. "Why are you here? Aerin didn't think you would be."

"Like I said, I needed a ride. I was at the Y. My friends went on to a party. I didn't want to go." He shrugged. "Besides, it's not the first Saturday night of my life I end up at one of Dad's things. Aerin's probably hiding in the kitchen making coffee. I'll get her." He turned away.

"Will."

He stopped. His head dropped and his hands remained in his pockets.

"Tell her I'll wait downstairs, okay? It was nice to see you."

He stood with his back to me a moment longer, then turned around slowly and moved in very close.

Oh, help. For a moment I wasn't sure I wouldn't do it all over again, even knowing how young he was. As we locked eyes, his chest rose and fell. I wanted to press my palm against the softness of the faded T shirt.

His whisper was harsh: "I knew that they'd just take you over."

>‹

The cold hard bench in the downstairs hall suited my mood. I tapped the broken branch of the ficus and it sagged even lower.

The elevator whirred as it rose to the second floor. A minute later it noisily landed and the door opened. Two older women walked out. They paused to button coats and tighten scarves. One of the ladies was tall and gaunt and wore a black pea coat. Her short gray bob was tucked behind her ears. A sparkly silver scarf hung to her knees, even after she wound it twice around her neck. She gave one scarf end a final toss over her shoulder. "Why do I do this?" she growled.

The other woman leaned a cane against the wall before buttoning her red coat. "Well, I always thought it was because you liked to hear him talk about health care." She laughed heartily. "Now can we please go to Louie's for a whiskey and some pool?"

Silver Scarf said something in a low, angry tone. Red Coat shook her head as she buttoned a final button over her broad chest. "Do not swear like that around me, Nan. Even when you aren't all mopey I don't much enjoy trailing after you down memory lane, and if you get angry, I won't again, not even if you promise me a pool game at the end of the night." Silver Scarf turned toward the door, again murmuring something. Red Coat grabbed her friend's arm. "Just do it, I say. Just go back now and tell him who you are."

Silver Scarf turned and made a face. "I'm no one."

"Will you listen to that!" Red Coat said. "'I'm no one.'" She pretended to wipe tears. "Poor me, poor me."

Silver Scarf put her hands on her hips and shifted her weight to one side. They glared at each other, then burst out laughing. Red Coat picked up her cane and used it to push her friend toward the door. Just as it opened and a cloud of cigarette smoke rolled in, Red Coat spotted me and smiled.

As soon as they'd left the building I sprang up from the bench and watched them walk away through the smokers.

Just tell him who you are. And who are you? I wondered. The elevator dinged its arrival, and I spun back around.

"Hanna, what's wrong?" Aerin said as she and Beth exited the elevator. "See a ghost?"

I again looked out the door. The women had disappeared. Not exactly a ghost, I thought. Just a woman who had something to say to your father. "No," I said softly. "Just thinking about something."

Aerin tipped her head toward her sister. "Beth's date canceled. Hope you don't mind if she joins us."

"Of course not, but maybe you'd—"

Before I could even finish the thought that they'd rather go without me, Beth blurted, "Son of a bitch. And he had the nerve to say he hoped I'd still introduce him to Dad. I should know better than to date lawyers."

Aerin sighed. "Then why do you? Always, lawyers. And let's not trouble Hanna with laments about your love life, because hers ain't so grand either."

Beth made a face at her sister. "Or yours."

Aerin shrugged. "Nothing new there." She tapped my shoulder. "Sorry you ran into Will. I really didn't expect he'd show tonight."

I held the door open for them. "Doesn't matter."

Beth hooked her arm through mine as we walked across the street to my car. "I hear you like to dance. I do too. This will be a lot better than spending the evening listening to some dickhead litigator talk about himself."

"Hanna," Aerin said, "would it surprise you to find out that my sister has trouble keeping boyfriends?"

"*My* sister," Beth said, still directing her conversation to me, "has minimal experience with dating, so you shouldn't listen to her on the subject. She's really only ever dated one guy, a U hockey player we didn't know about until it was all over."

Aerin started whistling.

"He dumped her," Beth continued, "the minute he found out she was fifteen. He was twenty-two."

"Fifteen, with twenty-two? What is with the people in your family?" I said as I unlocked the passenger doors.

"Oh, no," Beth said, getting into the front seat. "Not me. My mistakes are from my own age group."

Aerin smiled broadly at me as I walked around the car. She winked and said, "Jailbait."

"Maybe we shouldn't talk about boyfriends," I said when I got in and started the engine.

"Good idea," Beth said. "Hanna, this is great that you're going. For once I might have fun. Not only do I have someone to dance with, but I can have more than one beer now that I'm not driving Miss Crazy."

Aerin kicked the back of her sister's seat.

I must have made a little noise, because they both said, "What?"

I shook my head "Nothing, really. Just thinking a few good thoughts about being an only child."

>←

The band was nothing special. Good enough for dancing, though, so Beth and I spent a lot of time out on the floor. Aerin sat at a table in a dark corner, nursing a lemonade. Beth and I joined her when the band took a break.

"She flirts," Beth announced to her sister. "No doubt that's how she snared our infant brother. I swear she made eye contact with every male in the room."

I took a handful of pretzels from the bowl on the table. "Just trying to find someone to dance with who could keep up. Even a country two-step would be nice."

"I'm not that bad," Beth protested.

"Blame it on our parents," Aerin said. "None of us can dance, other than your basic freeform gyration. Will's pretty graceful, though. If you hadn't broken up so quick, I bet—"

I crushed the pretzel in my hand. "Would you please never mention him again?"

"That might be tough," Beth said. "He is our brother."

I emptied the pretzel crumbs onto the floor. When I looked up, they were both staring at me with the same serious expression.

"Wow," I said. "You two don't look at all alike, but you look exactly the same."

"Which makes no sense at all," Beth said as she signaled to the waitress for a fresh beer.

"What was your grandmother's first name?" I blurted.

Again, the twin looks. "Her name *is* Mary," said Beth.

Aerin reached for the pretzels. "I think she means Dad's mom."

"Naomi," Beth said when I nodded. "Why?"

Naomi? Silver Scarf's friend had called her Nan. Of course, names can be changed. "What did she look like?"

Aerin and Beth exchanged glances. "Don't know," Beth said. "We've never seen a picture and Dad's never said. I doubt if he remembers. Why?"

As I frantically thought for an answer that wouldn't seem crazy, Aerin asked, "What about your long-gone grandma, Hanna? Your mom's mom. What did she look like?"

Our eyes met. She smiled. "Remember—He Who Must Not Be Mentioned talked about everything." She turned to her sister. "Hanna also has a grandmother who ran out long ago and has never been heard from since."

The waitress arrived with a round of drinks. Aerin paid and gave her a huge tip. Beth sipped, then said, "I don't think of her as our grandmother. I don't think of her at all."

"Mine was tall and dark," I said, thinking about the pictures. "Sexy."

"There you go," Aerin said. "That's you."

I shook my head. "She was very slender. She had great hair." I sipped my Coke. "When I was waiting for you at the union hall tonight I heard these two women talking. From what they were saying I thought maybe one was your grandmother."

I eyed the sisters. Neither was smiling. "What were they saying?" Beth asked calmly. Ah, the lawyer.

"Nothing much. One was telling the other that she ought to go back upstairs and tell your dad who she was."

"She's probably just someone he's helped," Beth said. "His office helps a lot of people."

"She was kind of emotional."

"They get emotional," Beth said, "because what he does for them matters a lot." She picked up a pretzel. "Her name was Naomi Walker, Hanna. Before Dad ran for Congress the first time, there was a pretty thorough search for her. Naomi Walker died in a Salvation Army shelter in Chicago about twenty years ago."

"Case closed," Aerin said dryly. Beth flicked the pretzel at her.

"What a sad end," I said. "I'm sorry I mentioned it."

"What about your runaway granny?" Aerin said. "Is she alive?"

I nodded, wishing suddenly that I could reverse time and take the conversation back to a different subject— even talking about Will would be better than spilling it to these two. "I think so. I know that she was living in Spain a couple of years ago. I just dug that up on the Internet." I took a long deep drink. "I sent her a letter last night."

"Ah," Beth said. "Then today you imagine you run into ours. Makes sense. You had grandmas on the brain."

Aerin leaned forward. "Why, Hanna? I'm sorry, but I'm curious about, oh, I don't know—the story."

"Be careful what you say," Beth said as she lifted her glass. "It will get used in a song."

Aerin ignored her. "You and your mom seem so great together, so why do you suppose you suddenly want more?"

My eyes darted between the disparate sisters sitting side by side and watching me.

Because you've fallen in love with another family, I heard Mom whisper. "No," I said softly.

"No what?" Aerin asked.

I leaned back, took a breath. "No particular reason, I guess. Just curious, like you say." I looked away, anxious to avoid their interest. "Uh-oh—talk about curious; I see three farm boys checking us out."

Right away the mood at the table changed and chilled. Beth moved to a different chair, blocking Aerin from public view.

"Can't I even talk to them?" I said. "I drive you two forty miles to a country bar on a winter night and I don't get to talk to the locals?" I smiled at the tallest of the farm boys before turning back to the sisters. "I say we pair up according to height."

Aerin laughed, but Beth frowned. I said to her, "Do they look like lawyers? They do not. So why don't you take a chance?" Still no smile. "Beth, it's just for a dance or two. If anyone catches on to Aerin, we'll leave right away."

She shook her head. "Hanna, you have no idea what sort of things people have said to her when they've discovered who she is. I'm just trying to protect her from that."

"It's not as if I want anything to happen either, but it was her idea to come and— Why are we talking about her like she's not here?" I turned to the younger sister. "What do you want to do?"

Aerin's eyes jumped back and forth between us. She leaned toward me. "Did Will by any chance ever tell you that Beth turned down the chance to clerk for a Supreme Court justice so she could live in Minnesota and be company for her damaged sister? Or did he tell you how she's never once complained when I wake her in the middle of the night because I need to talk? Or—"

"Aerin, stop it," Beth said. "Let's just go. I'm sorry, Hanna."

Aerin reached across the small round table and tucked a strand of hair behind her sister's ear. "I wouldn't mind dancing with a cute farm boy."

Beth said, "I don't know. The last time . . ." She shook her head.

I said, "Trust me." I lifted a hand and waved to the guys. As soon as they saw me they made congratulatory noises to each other, consulted, then started our way. "Quick," I said to Aerin, "what's your middle name?"

"Sylvia."

"Sylvia," I murmured. "Sylvia . . . Callahan."

Aerin lifted her sister's beer glass. "A fine name." She sipped.

The boys pulled up chairs. "From the Cities?" the tall one said.

"That's right," I replied. "We heard the band was good. I'm Hanna. My cousins"—I pointed to each of the sisters—"Beth and Sylvia. Do you like to dance?"

The tall guy said, "Who doesn't." He looked at Aerin. "You seem familiar."

Before either sister could make a move, I said, "Of course she does."

"Hanna," Beth murmured. Aerin put a hand on her sister's arm. She and I exchanged looks. I could tell she was curious. I could see her thinking: What happens next?

I said, "I bet you guys have been to the Minnesota State Fair, right?" They nodded. "She was the dairy queen thing a couple of years ago."

"Princess Kay of the Milky Way?" the shortest boy said, obviously awed. Beth slumped in her seat, no doubt just then realizing that if we stayed, he'd be her date for the rest of the evening.

"That's probably why she's familiar," I said. All three guys stared at Aerin and nodded, believing it.

"This cousin," said Aerin, pointing at her sister, "was a runner-up two years before me." The guys focused on Beth, who was now hiding a smile by drinking beer. "Isn't that right, Cousin Beth?"

Beth wiped the foam with the back of her hand. "That's right, but it was no big deal being runner-up. I mean, yes, I got a sash and got to be in a couple of parades, but you had your sculpture done in butter." She rose. "You're always showing me up, Sylvia." She held out her hand to the short guy. "Band's getting ready. Want to dance?"

Aerin tossed back the rest of her sister's beer, rose, and led the medium guy out to the floor just as the first notes shook the room.

Tall Guy smiled at me. "I hope you're up to this," I said, "because women in my family are demon dancers; men have actually died in our arms."

We wore out more than one set of dance partners. They really started dropping once I persuaded the band to try adding a little Latin rhythm to their numbers. By closing time—with their wives cheering from the sidelines—only a trio of middle-aged guys were keeping up with us. It wouldn't surprise me to hear someday that the men in west central Wisconsin were still talking about Hanna, Beth, and Sylvia—the Callahan cousins.

It was a fun night, and it would have been great to do it again, but I was under absolutely no illusion that I'd found two new best friends; after all, Aerin and Beth were older, they had lives, they had each other.

It was Mom who finally heard from Aerin. Two weeks after the night at the bar she got a package from her with a CD, some sheets of music, and a short note. Mom read it to me as we ate a frozen-dinner meal together:

> *Claudia—*
> *I've headed to Tucson to visit friends. The Minnesota gray was getting to me. I reworked some of the pieces and made a recording. I've included the music in case you want it performed live. Just piano and cello—a little austere, but then* Our Town *is set in New England, so that's probably fine. I'd appreciate it very much if you didn't make copies of the CD or tell anyone that I composed the music. Use a pseudonym, if you get pushed. Hanna knows what name to use. Oh, the last track has nothing to do with* Our Town. *Something Hanna started got me going on that one, so I thought I'd toss it in.*
> *Good luck with the show.*

Love, Aerin.

P.S. Your daughter can really dance—she taught at least a dozen people how to cha-cha-cha.

Mom opened the jewel case and pulled out the liner notes Aerin had hand-written. She handed them to me. I scanned the titles until I reached the last one: "Butter Girl Blues."

6
Chasing Ghosts

The second-biggest snowstorm I've ever experienced happened on a Halloween when I was in elementary school. As I waited for the school bus that morning, it was balmy and no one wore coats. By the time I returned home in the afternoon, there was a fierce wind, cold air, and a blinding snowfall that continued for two days until thirty inches had piled up.

I'd sprained an ankle earlier in the week, so Dad had to pull me on a sled when we went trick-or-treating that night. Most of the houses in our neighborhood have steps going up from the sidewalk, so he was the one who actually went and knocked on doors while I'd wave from the sled and shout, "Trick or treat." Dad and I made a pretty pathetic picture; we brought home a huge amount of candy.

The biggest snowstorm began the Saturday night *Our Town* closed. The show was terrific and the music by "Sylvia Callahan" was perfect, but the audience was still restless. I watched with Mom from the back of the theater, and we spotted lots of people checking watches. As soon as the house lights went up, there was a wild rush to the parking lot. Minnesotans are pretty skilled at dealing with snow, but even we freak when the TV weather geeks predict that thirty-five inches of the stuff will soon be clogging streets and highways.

Mom and I live just a few miles from Whipple. By the time we left the school it was really coming down. It took us almost an hour to drive home and it took three tries to get the car off the street and up onto the driveway.

We rushed to get in pajamas. Mom was in her bathrobe staring out the living room window when I brought her a mug of hot chocolate. "Another great show," I said. We tapped mugs, then turned off lights and pulled chairs up to the window to watch the storm. "This is perfect," she murmured. "The whole world will slow down for a few days."

"Ha," I said as I spooned a marshmallow out of my mug. "You don't work in retail."

>‹

Eight o'clock Monday morning, while most of the Twin Cities was still digging out, I was on duty in swimwear, hanging merchandise brought in for a big sale. By the time the store opened to customers at nine thirty, there were already a few office workers browsing on their breaks. By eleven the department was actually busy, filled mostly with moms and children, all obviously stir-crazy from being cooped up for too long by the storm. By noon the office workers returned. Apparently it had been a tough put-on-the-pounds winter for everyone, because I was running nonstop between racks and changing rooms bringing horrified customers larger sizes.

By one o'clock I was desperate for a break. As soon as my manager gave me the nod, I left.

The buildings in the central part of downtown Minneapolis are connected by skyways. Once you get inside any one building, you don't have to go outside to get to another one, even if it's blocks away. The routes to go from place to place aren't all that direct, but they're snow-free and warm. The system cuts through the store on the second floor, channeling traffic through the men's department. I rode the escalator down, joined the flow of purposeful skyway traffic, and headed toward the food court.

I bought a four-berry smoothie. I stood in a glass-walled skyway over Nicollet Mall and drank my lunch. The street and sidewalks below were deserted except for the occasional bus. Snow was piled up on each corner. A car drove through a distant intersection, fishtailed, then straightened and sped off. Moments later a police sedan followed, its siren muted, but its lights rippling bright colors.

A trio of girls burst out of a store down below. Talking and laughing, they linked arms and began stomping their way through the snow. One spotted me watching and said something to the others. They halted their march to wave—six arms flailing away with exuberant best-friends-having-fun energy.

I tossed my unfinished smoothie into a trash can and headed back to work.

Back in the store, I walked like the other drones, though my eyes were glued to a piece of puke-green yarn clinging to the hip of the beige skirt on the woman right ahead of me. I kept pace, all the while wondering if I should stop her and tell her about the offending yarn, ignore it, or gamble and try to pluck it off myself without being noticed.

Take a chance, Hanna.

I drew closer, matched my stride to hers, reached out—

Someone grabbed my hand and yanked me out of the stream of people. "Are you nuts?" Beth Walker asked.

It took me a moment to recognize her, maybe because I was intent on shaking the feeling back into my hand or maybe because every other time I'd seen her she was dressed a bit more casually, to say the least. Today she was wearing an expensive-looking suit, a silk blouse, and a terrific necklace. "Hi, Beth. You know, you are the perfect advertisement for a career in law."

"And you were just about to get in deep trouble, Hanna."

"She had some yarn on her skirt. I was trying to pick it off."

She smiled. "I saw it. You could have just told her. You know who that woman is? The county's chief criminal prosecutor. If she felt you touching her, you might have been slapped with an assault charge. Lucky I spotted you when I did." She tugged on my arm. "I just saved your ass, so now you can do something for me." She tipped her head.

Will and his mother watched from deep inside the men's department. Ms. Callahan smiled and waved. Will looked like he wanted to disappear.

"I don't think so," I said when I finally caught my breath. "My lunch break is almost over."

"This should only take a minute. We need your opin-

ion. Actually, they need your opinion; I know I'm right."
Before I could come up with another excuse, Beth
Walker—inches shorter and pounds lighter—once again
had me by the arm and was dragging me along.

"How lucky Beth spotted you," Ms. Callahan said as we
approached. "We can't agree on the tie. You have the
deciding vote, Hanna."

I risked a glance at Will. "New suit?" Dumb question,
of course, because there were all sorts of tags hanging
from it. He obviously thought it was dumb too, because
his only response was to shoot me his practiced-on-sisters
withering look. "It's nice," I said.

He looked at his feet.

"This Saturday is my stepfather's birthday celebration,"
Ms. Callahan said. "We're all going to the opera and that
calls for a suit, don't you think?" She held out three ties
for me to examine. "And maybe a shave?"

Will's beard looked as feeble as ever. I put my hands
behind my back and turned to study the ties. "I'd better
not get involved in that argument. The maroon is very
nice."

Beth made a happy noise. "Ha. Told you."

"But the yellow one looks better with the dark brown
wool."

Ms. Callahan tapped her daughter's shoulder. "I win."

The third tie was a medium blue with narrow green
stripes. I lifted it from her arm and held it up to his

neck. "But this one would look best on Will." He raised
his eyes to meet mine; they gave away nothing. He was
cool as ice. I handed the tie back to his mother. "The
suit he's got on is very handsome, but he'd look even
better in navy."

In a flash Beth and her mom were going through the navy suits. Will leaned back against a display table and again stared down. "We were almost done," he said softly. "Now we'll be here at least another hour." His hair fell across his face as he looked down. Fortunately he tucked it back before I could.

"I need to get back to work," I said. "It was nice to see you." I waited for him to say something else. When he kept quiet, I turned and walked away.

><

In quick succession we had three more heavy snowfalls, which made a grand total of fifty-five inches in about two weeks. Each storm did a better job of slowing down life. By the third snowfall people were doing half-assed jobs shoveling, and someone at city hall had apparently decided that all Minneapolitans were capable of climbing over the snow piles that had been left at intersections. To make it worse, we got a dose of frigid air after each dump, and that meant any snow that hadn't been totally cleared was now frozen rock solid.

The fourth cold snap was the worst. It was like the bottom fell out of the weather god's thermometer. It was especially demoralizing because it was already early March. Even for Minnesota that's way too late for insane cold.

I survived by looking fashion stupid every time I went out: clunky boots, wind pants over my work pants, down parka, leather choppers for mittens. At least the scarf and hat matched; Mom had knit them both.

On day three of the cold snap, a Saturday, I arrived at work in a foul mood after getting off the bus and promptly stumbling over a snowbank in front of at least two dozen people.

"Thank goodness you're here," Diana said as soon as I walked into the staff room. "I am so glad to see you."

I sat on a chair. "When am I ever not here?" I wiggled a foot and the clunky boot fell off. "I suddenly have a really bad feeling about the night."

"Carol and Jo both called in sick. How do you feel about working until closing?"

Saturday night, but where else would I go? What else would I do? I pulled off the other boot. Snow dropped from the sole in globs that landed on the floor in interesting patterns.

If tea leaves can have meaning, why wouldn't it be possible to tell fortunes by the way crap falls off your shoes?

I pasted on a bright smile for Diana and nodded. She patted her heart and hurried back out to the sales floor. "I knew I could count on you!" she called over her shoulder.

Of course you can, I thought. Everyone else has a life. I gave the boot a final shake. A snow clump fell off the fake fur trim, hit the floor, and exploded in all directions.

>‹

Business was slow and the day dragged. Diana and I took turns taking leisurely breaks. When I got back from dinner I waved her away and took command of the deserted swimwear department. After about three minutes of staring at bikini-clad mannequins, I picked up the phone and called Cate.

"You?" she said. "We all decided you were dead. What's the occasion?"

I decided to blow past the less-than-warm greeting. "Extreme boredom at work. I'm also tired of the sound of my own voice. Any chance you and D'Neeka need a third wheel tonight? I'm off at nine thirty."

"Oh crap," I said as her silence went on way too long. "What's up?"

"People are sort of hanging at Maura's tonight." When *my* silence went on too long, she said, "I heard that she busted a secret of yours. Don't know what it was, though maybe I can guess from the stuff that was going around for a while. Hey, don't swear at me, okay?"

"Sorry." A customer strolled in and started flipping through cover-ups. "Gotta go," I whispered.

"You could come, you know. Everyone would be glad to see you."

"Not a chance."

"I think you're right to be mad at her. But this long silence with everyone is kind of a scorched-earth tactic, Hanna."

"Maybe I figured you were all taking her side because no one's called me lately."

"No one's taking sides. And if you haven't heard from people maybe it's because you ignored messages and you didn't answer e-mail. People quit trying, okay?" She took a drink of something. "It would be good to see you. I'm sorry I haven't called; that was wrong. D'Neeka and I will meet you at Dunn Bros at ten."

"I don't want to be a pity date." The customer approached the counter with a peach robe in her hands and a question on her face. "Go to Maura's."

The bus home was almost empty. I rode past my stop

and got off two blocks later at the coffee shop. I'd blown off Cate's offer of company and didn't really expect her to be there, but maybe there'd be music, or some other friend. At the very least there'd be decent hot chocolate before I headed home to my now standard Saturday night fare: an empty house, TV, bed.

I stood in the shadows just outside the bright window of the crowded coffee shop. Maura and Kelsey sat with D'Neeka and Cate at a small table near the front. No one looked happy. I went in and walked straight to them. I suppose everything showed on my face, because Kelsey's mouth dropped open when she spotted me. "Bloody ambush," I said loudly. I crouched by Maura. "Have you figured it out yet?"

"I know why you're pissed, if that's what you mean. You made that clear weeks ago, Hanna."

"I poured it all out and you treated what I told you like cheap middle school gossip." I stood. "Too damn bad we're not talking, because now there's a whole lot more I think you'd find interesting."

Kelsey rose and reached for me. "Hanna, please."

I said, "Hey, how's it going with Spence?" Her hand dropped. I turned and hurried out of the coffee shop. "Bloody ambush, bloody ambush," I whispered again and again until I was practically marching to the sound of the words. I started jogging. Bloody freaking ambush.

They beat me to the house. Maura's car was in the driveway. I turned around and kept walking.

I was so bundled up that the cold didn't hit until I reached the lake, where the north wind rushed across the frozen expanse and slammed into me. I pulled my hood down to my eyebrows and pulled my scarf up to my eyes. I walked down the steps, across the playground, and out onto the ice.

Heavy breathing echoed loudly in the cavern of my hood. Snow and ice crunched underfoot. Crystals formed on my eyelashes and blurred all the lights. I stopped walking and cleared my vision by pressing hands on my eyes. The apartment buildings on the west side of the lake glowed. "That way!" I shouted and pointed. "The diner is over there! Go that way to death!"

I turned around slowly. Where had it happened? Here? I stomped. Rock solid. Lucky they found Derek when they did; otherwise, he'd be down there still, locked in the lake until spring.

Car lights streamed by on the parkway. Was one of them Maura's? Could anyone see me? Would anyone wonder or worry? Would anyone hear if I screamed?

I lay on the ice and looked at the dark sky. No North Star tonight. "What the hell do I do now?" I shouted. "Where do I go?"

Cold seeped through the layers of clothing. I sat up, unwrapped my scarf, and pushed back the hood. Wind slid down my neck.

Were you this cold, Lindsey? And what did it feel like to leave him behind?

What froze first on your face: lake water or tears?

I unzipped my parka and shook it off my shoulders. This cold?

I hugged my knees as tears hardened and burned on my cheeks. So cold.

Maura's car was gone when I returned to the house. I looked up and down the street. Were they parked and waiting? I hurried in and slammed the door behind me.

Mom and Charles were cuddling on the couch and watching TV. She bolted up. "What in the world? You look frozen to death."

I pushed back my hood. "Why are you home so early?"

"We went to a movie instead of the club. We just got back. Hanna, what's wrong?"

They must have missed Maura and the others, so it was probably safe to go with the lies: "I waited twenty minutes for a bus," I croaked, "then the damn heater hardly worked."

They bolted into action and the result was sweet: Within five minutes I was free of the winter gear, wrapped in a fleecy blanket, and holding a mug of hot chocolate. Then Mom made the biggest gesture of all: She offered me the TV remote. I shook my head. "Think I'll take a hot shower and then disappear into my room. If anyone calls or drops by, I'm in bed."

Mom looked appropriately puzzled. After all, how long had it been since anyone had called or dropped in? I said, "Good night." I stopped halfway up the stairs. "It would be really stupid for anyone to go out in this cold unless he absolutely had to. As far as I'm concerned, Charles, you don't have to, even if tomorrow is Sunday. Stick around for once and get in on the fun. Hell, join us every week."

The hot shower helped some, but I still felt pretty deep-chilled. I layered a blanket over my bathrobe and pajamas and sat at the computer. Just as I expected: fresh e-mails from Maura and Kelsey.

Maura: *What just happened? Are you okay?*

Kelsey: *I don't know if I'm worried about you or pissed at you.*

Me to them: *Don't be worried, but go ahead and be pissed. After all, that's pretty much how I feel, to say the least.*

Then I went ahead and said a whole lot more—a couple of paragraphs of a whole lot more. When I finally hit the "Send" button my hands were shaking.

Ten years of friendship blown apart. Two kids dead. Sex with a fourteen-year-old boy.

Hell of a winter, Hanna. *Everything* I'd touched had gone bad.

The corner of a sketchbook jutted out of a drawer. I yanked it out and opened it to a drawing of Lindsey frozen on the snow. I turned to the next page: Derek floating in icy water. I flipped through the pad. Lindsey. Derek. Lindsey. Derek.

Death, death, and more death.

My eyes landed on the Hawaii drawings near my desk. These were the worst of all, I thought. Simple-minded postcards from paradise, pure pastel froth practically decaying with a sickening sweetness, all of them about as meaningful as a potato chip jingle. What was the point?

I ripped down the pastels and tossed them into a desk drawer. Then I logged onto my website manager file, selected the home page, hit the left arrow—*zing*—and sucked it out of cyberspace.

Zing. Derek under ice—gone.

Zing. Lindsey on the snow—gone.

Zing. Tall boy and red snow—gone.

Zing. Zing. Zing. I kept going until every page was gone, vanished without a trace.

I wasn't finished. I cleared supplies off the desk and table, sweeping everything into a cardboard box that I crammed under the bed. I folded up the easel and put it behind a dresser. Canvases went into the closet and drawings got rolled up and slipped into a cardboard tube.

The bare walls looked good.

>‹

I slept until eleven. In deference to the male visitor I assumed was still in the house, I dressed before going downstairs. Mom was reading the newspaper on the sofa. Charles stood at the window.

"Morning," I said with cheer that I hoped wasn't too bogus. "Sorry I was such a grouch last night. I guess I was tired from work. Do you suppose it's still cold out there?"

"Already warmed up to five below," said Charles. "There's a boy clearing the ice on your sidewalk."

Mom and I joined him at the window and watched the hooded figure hack away. "I'm glad I left the ice chopper on the stoop yesterday," Mom said. "But who is it?"

As if he'd heard her, Will turned around and waved.

He came inside when he was done. "It's really cold. So weird for March," he said as he pulled off his boots. "Your walk was nasty. I almost fell. You could get sued." He smiled at Mom. "Not by me."

"You shaved," I said. "Looks good."

He made a face as he rubbed his cold-reddened cheeks.

I introduced him to Charles, then led him to the kitchen. Someone had made muffins and Will quickly devoured four. "What are you doing here?" I said as he stared at the remaining two muffins. I took one and peeled off the paper.

"Hi to you too. Any chance I could have some juice?"

While I was pouring him a glass, Mom came in. "Will, what size shoe do you wear?"

My laughter only confused him more. "She's into knitting socks these days," I said. "She must think you deserve a pair for clearing the ice."

"Twelve," he said.

"Color?" she asked.

"Blue," he said firmly. He gave me a warning look.

"I'll make some for Aerin too," Mom said as she walked away. "Green, I think, to match her eyes. Be sure to leave your address so I can mail them."

"Mail them?" Will whispered to me. "She absolutely doesn't want me to come by again, does she?"

"She'll probably have them done before you get the chance. You didn't answer my question. What are you doing here?"

"I needed to ask you something."

"You have my number and e-mail."

"I wanted to do it in person." He shifted his weight onto one hip and pulled a folded newspaper clipping out of his back pocket. "This was in the paper. Today's that girl's birthday."

I pushed back. Sat stiffly erect. Felt the cold returning.

"Her parents are having an open house all afternoon,"

he said. "I'm not free until three or so, but I thought maybe I'd go then. Do you want to? I—" He finally noticed my expression and stopped talking.

"Will, no. I really don't want to do that."

He chewed on his lip. "I still see her, Hanna."

I took his hand. "Your grandmother's a psych nurse, right? Talk to her."

He made a face. "I just came from there. I crashed at her house last night after a party. She's the one who noticed this in the paper this morning and thought I should do it. She offered to go with me, but I thought maybe you . . ." He crumpled the clipping.

"I'm sorry, Will. I just want to make it all fade away."

He pulled his hand away from mine. "Is that the trick, Hanna? Pretend nothing happened and hope it all fades away? Well, I don't think it's right to forget that something happened."

"I went to the lake last night, Will. I went out on the ice. It doesn't fade away. Nothing does. I can't face her parents."

He didn't seem surprised. He even nodded. "I've walked out on the lake. I even . . ." He leaned forward. "Once I even laid down on the snow where I found her. Just wondering, you know? Is that too weird?"

"No," I said softly.

He glanced toward the other room, then reached for my hand and lifted it to his lips. "Sorry," he said as I abruptly pulled away. "Last time. Promise." He played with a loose yarn on the frayed hem of his sweater. "Dumb idea, really, to go to that party. I don't care if my grandma thinks it would be good for me to get it out, I can't imagine what I would say to the parents. That I'm the guy who found her and then ran away?" He shook his head. "Dumb idea," he repeated. He forced a small smile. "But it wasn't the only reason I came by. I thought I should apologize."

"For what?"

"For being such a prick when I saw you at Dad's meeting and at the store."

"You were ambushed. No one ever does the right thing when that happens." I glanced toward the living room. It was mother-daughter day, but with Charles here everything had changed. "Will, I'd like to get out of the house. Do you want to go grab lunch or something? But we're just hanging out, okay? That's got to be clear."

When he slumped, he looked like a heartbroken little boy. "I can't. Not until later anyway." A fast mood change swept across his face. "Hey, maybe you want to come with me."

"Where?"

"Another one of Dad's town meetings. I really don't go to that many, but he provides a free lunch at this one and they always need people to help serve." He lowered his voice. "Maybe she'll be there and you can talk to her."

"Who?"

"The woman you saw. You know, Aerin says that they never proved it absolutely that the woman who died in Chicago was our grandmother."

It took me a minute to recover. "Do you and Aerin talk about everything? Are you like the one weird boy in the world whose best friend is his big sister?"

"My best friend's a guy named Ben. He's a year ahead of me at South and—"

"Ah, a sophomore."

"—he plays center field."

"Does Ben know about me?"

Will smiled. "A little bit. You might call it a rough sketch. Does your best friend know about me?"

Best friends, plural, I thought. And let's make it past tense. I held his stare with my own as I nodded, quickly deciding to mislead rather than go into details. "A rough sketch."

His stocking foot tapped against mine. "So, will you come?"

"Fine, but we're just hanging out. And I'm not looking for that woman."

→←

The Wedge Community Center was packed. As we entered the building, the strong smell of cafeteria food hit like familiar but noxious fumes.

"I know that smell," I said. "Salisbury steak."

He nodded. "Are you hungry?"

I got another whiff of the cafeteria. "Not especially."

"Good. Then we'll just get to work." He led me to the kitchen, showed me where to hang my coat, and introduced me to people. "Most everyone in here works in Dad's Minneapolis office or is a volunteer from one of the groups that support him," he explained. He paused on the tour and lightly punched the shoulder of a young woman talking heatedly on a cell phone. "This is Lisa. She's his press officer. You won't see her in an apron."

Everyone seemed to know and like Will. If anyone was curious about him showing up with a girl, no one gave it away, but then everyone but Lisa was busy serving food.

I washed my hands, accepted an apron, and took a place behind one of the mashed potato bins. Will whispered, "I'm going to go check in with Dad. I'll be back. Then you can cruise around and look for her."

"No rush," I said. "I'm here to work, not to chase ghosts."

I'd stepped back from the counter to let a volunteer dump more mashed potatoes into the serving vat when I noticed that Lisa had finally finished her phone call. She stared at me as she closed the phone and slipped it into her pocket. I gave her a smile and turned back to the diner waiting for her potatoes.

Lisa came over. "I know Will told me who you are, but I was getting chewed out by someone and it didn't register. Are you one of the Sierra Club volunteers?"

"Her name's Hanna," the server next to me said. "Friend of Will's."

Lisa studied my face. Again I offered up a smile; I didn't want a bad report going back to her boss. She glanced at her watch. "Damn. Mark had better stop schmoozing and start taking questions soon. We've got to be at the VA hospital in two hours."

I spotted the congressman moving among the diners. He was shaking hands, chatting, and listening. "Looks like he's having fun."

Lisa sighed and moved toward the kitchen exit. "That's the problem," she said.

She corralled Will's dad and guided him toward a microphone. Everyone in the kitchen quit talking as he began speaking. Except for the scraping of utensils on plates, the dining hall was also quiet. The final few people moved silently through the serving line. When the last one had a plate, a volunteer reached up and pulled a wide shutter down to the counter.

Following the lead of the other workers, I picked up my potato bin and hauled it back to a work island in the kitchen. I was scooping leftovers into a big plastic tub when Will came up behind me and whispered, "Take a break and go look around. I'll finish up."

"I told you: I'm not chasing after a dead woman."

"Fine, then take a break and go listen to your congressman."

I had just settled into a rear corner of the dining hall and was starting to tune in to Will's dad when I saw the woman rising from a table on the far side of the room. Her fuchsia sweater caught my eye. She put on her coat and turned to leave. I gave her a brief head start, then I sauntered toward the building's foyer.

Hello, Nan, I thought. Or can I call you Naomi?

She was studying bus schedules that were posted in a display case when I caught up. I stood alongside and peered through the dirty glass. "It's hard to read, it's so smeared," I said. She didn't answer. She put her finger on the glass and dragged it down the list of times for the inbound 17A. She pulled gloves out of her pocket and one dropped on the slushy floor. I dove to pick it up, and we nearly bumped heads. I held out the glove, and she glared at me.

She didn't have a happy face: There was a jagged scar between her two thick eyebrows; her lips were thin and cracked; her eyes were red and wet. I could see that she'd once been a pretty woman, but even so, there was absolutely nothing about her that resembled Will's handsome dad.

I'm nuts, I thought as I stared.

She grabbed the glove out of my hand. Just as she turned to leave, her eyes widened. "Oh, damn, oh damn," she muttered. "Too cruel." She covered her mouth, stifling a soft moan, then hurried from the building. I turned. Beth Walker stood scowling in the doorway leading to the dining hall.

I raised my hand. "Hi there, Beth. Sorry. Gotta go."

I moved to follow the lady, but a hand on my arm held me. "Why leave so soon?" Beth said. "Aren't you interested in my dad's thoughts on defense spending?"

I pulled, but Beth tightened her grip. "Please, Beth. Just give me a second." I covered her hand with my own and peeled the fingers loose one by one. As I finally released my arm, I heard the wheezing sound of a bus slowing to a stop at the corner outside the center. "Beth, I swear—unless we're on a dance floor, if you ever grab me again, I'll beat you up. I'm bigger; I know I could do it."

She stepped back. "Sorry. Who was that, Hanna? And please don't tell me it's our mystery grandmother. I'd hate to think a smart girl like you—"

Will ran out of the dining hall. He pulled up when he saw his sister and then slid on the slushy wet floor. "Oh shit," he said. "I didn't think you were coming today." He looked back and forth between Beth and me a few times before his curiosity got to him. "Was that the woman, Hanna? I've seen her before. Did you talk to her?"

"Oh, man!" Beth hit her hip with a fist and bit down on her lip.

Will said, "So who the hell is she, Beth?" His sister shrugged.

"She got pretty upset when you appeared, Beth," I said.

A wave of laughter and applause spilled out of the dining hall. Beth pointed at a concrete bench at the far end of the foyer. "Sit." We sat. She stood in front of us. "Hanna, our grandmother—if you insist on calling her that—is dead."

I looked at my hands.

She sat next to me. I wiggled closer to Will to make room on the bench. "I don't know who she is, Hanna, but she's not our dad's mother."

"No one knows for sure that she's dead, Beth," Will said. "Aerin said so."

Beth pulled out a tissue and blew her nose. "I have such a nasty cold. Hope you don't catch it. Can you believe this weather in March? I talked to Aerin last night, by the way. It was ninety in Tucson. She mentioned that she'd done some music for your mom's play. That's so like her not to tell anyone. I wish she had. I'd have gone to the show."

"It added a lot. Mom was thrilled."

Beth blew her nose again. She wadded the tissue and made a bull's-eye toss into a waste can in the corner. "How much do you know about our dad, Hanna?"

I shifted so I could face her. "Not much. Will told me that he grew up in foster homes. Otherwise, all I know is that he's a terrific congressman. Been in Congress forever."

"Since he was thirty-two. He was first elected to the state legislature when he was only twenty-seven. We have this family friend who took him under his wing when Dad was about twenty, just after he got out of the army.

Rob helped him through college and law school and got him launched into politics. He pretty much groomed Dad for a public life."

"Sounds like a good friend," I said.

"He is. He's almost a grandfather to us, really, and my uncle and I even work for his firm. But no matter how close he is to Dad and the family, there was no way Rob and his political pals were going to risk any bad surprises popping up during a campaign."

"Like an embarrassing long-lost mother?"

Beth nodded. "As I told you the night you first saw this woman, before Dad ran for Congress everything that could possibly be a problem was checked out. That's when they found out Naomi Walker was dead."

Will stood and glared at his sister. "There was never any medical proof that the woman they found was his mother. They didn't dig up her body or do tests or anything. No one knows for sure."

"Will, she's dead. Dad thinks so, Rob thinks so, and I do too." She rose. "Have you heard from your grandmother, Hanna?"

Another bull's-eye hit. I shook my head.

"Well, maybe there hasn't been time enough yet to get a letter back from Spain. I hope you get one." She squeezed my shoulder and returned to the dining hall.

Will sat down. "You look like crap. And what's that about Spain?"

"Don't ask. I am so stupid, Will. Why have I suddenly gotten so stupid? Once again I have totally humiliated myself with the Walker family."

"That's crazy. I dragged you here. I sent you out to

look for the woman. Was she really upset when she saw Beth?"

"Let's just drop it."

"What happened, Hanna?" When I didn't answer, he said, "I'll look for her the next time Dad has a public meeting. I'm going to talk to her."

"Don't bother," I said glumly. "It's all fantasy. You heard your sister."

"Fine, it's a fantasy. But the woman's not, and now I'm curious: Who the hell is she?"

><

When I got home, Charles was gone and Mom was knitting with blue yarn. "You left rather abruptly," she said without looking up. "How much do I get to know?" Her lips continued moving silently, counting stitches.

She'd get an edited version, of course. "There's not much to tell. I went with him to help at one of his dad's town meetings. It was a packed house. I served mashed potatoes and saw Will's oldest sister again. Can we talk?"

She set down her knitting and fixed a smile. Never in my memory had she passed up an opportunity for mother-daughter intimacy, especially if I'd initiated it, but apprehension was all over her face. "About Will or Charles?" she said slowly.

"Neither. I have a confession."

She stared at the half-finished sock on the needle, then placed it all in a basket. She looked up at me, obviously anticipating the worst.

I sat beside her on the sofa. "I wrote to your mother last month. I read the letter from the law firm that was with the photos in your desk. I found the law firm's current address on the Internet and sent the letter there for them to forward."

Her head jerked back and her jaw dropped open. Stunned. After a moment the juices resumed flowing and I saw a spark of something in her eye. "And have you gotten a reply?" she said tersely.

"No. Probably because I just won't, but maybe because she's living in Spain, I think, and with all the forwarding there hasn't been time." While she absorbed that, I got the printout of Carolyn Cortland's obituary from my room. "Spain," I said again and gave the paper to Mom.

She read it through quickly and handed it back. "I never thought it would be all that tough to track her down. I just never wanted to. I'm not surprised that you're curious, Hanna, but I wish—"

I touched her arm. "Please don't say I'm doing it because I've fallen for Will's family and now I'm unhappy with ours. I just want to know more—about her, yes, but maybe really about you and me."

"If that's so, then be careful about looking in the wrong place. Try a mirror, darling; not dark corners."

I made space between us. "God, Mom. That's a load of psych-babble. I can tell you were married to a shrink way too long." Right away I wanted it back.

"No, Hanna," she said sharply. "It was not too long."

"Mom," I said softly. "I shouldn't have—"

She raised her hand, cutting me off angrily. "You want to know about her? Fine. *This* is what I remember: One evening in May when I was three years old I kissed her good night and when I woke up the next morning she was gone and it felt like my life had vanished. After that, every year on her birthday and at Christmas I sent a letter to her parents' address in Atlanta. I was too young to write at first, but I'd scribble my name on a picture I'd drawn. And every year on my birthday and at Christmas I hoped and waited to get something from her. Nothing. Ever. All that wishing and hoping stopped when I was ten and Dad got that letter you read. I never wrote again."

"Not even when you were married?" Mom shook her head. "When I was born?"

"By then I absolutely didn't care. I didn't even think of her."

"On the day I was born, you didn't think about your own mother?"

"I was too happy."

She wasn't happy now. She tilted her head, studying me as she decided what to say. Then: "You knew your grandfather was her geology professor?"

"No. One of the many details we haven't discussed." I flipped over Carolyn Cortland's obit and reached for a pencil. "What do you say we make a list of them."

"Knock it off, would you," she snapped. "This is hard enough for me without the attitude." I dropped the pencil. "Since you're suddenly interested in family history, you may as well know that your grandfather seduced and slept with one of his students and got her pregnant. Way back then it would have been typical for a young woman to go away somewhere to deal with that sort of pregnancy, to a home for unwed mothers or maybe a relative's. Then she'd give up the child. The way I came to understand it, my mother—" She licked her lips; obviously the phrase left a bad taste. "—simply took a little bit longer and traveled an indirect path to arrive at that same decision. She gave up her child, like so many women have felt they had to do. She did what she thought was best."

"Mom, that doesn't add up. I've seen the honeymoon picture—they look like they're ready to rip swimsuits off each other. You can't tell me they weren't ever happy, because it's obvious they were."

"I'm sure they were. Your grandfather was—is—a charming man. You've seen the other two pictures. What's obvious about those?"

"Not so happy. Mom, is there a reason there are only those three photos? I mean, it would make more sense if there were none of her. And one has brown marks, like from a fire. I thought maybe Grandpa—"

Her face had paled. She pressed her lips together.

"Oh, I am so incredibly dense. You did it."

She nodded slightly. "My tenth birthday. I was furious about once again not hearing from her. Dad had saved all the photos; there were quite a few. After he went to bed that night I ripped them out of albums and started a fire in the kitchen sink. He smelled the smoke and arrived in time to salvage those three. He put them away somewhere. I didn't see them again for years. He sent them to me right about the time you were born."

"I'm so sorry I started all this, Mom. I didn't do it to hurt you."

"I hope . . ." she whispered, then her eyes lost focus. "I really do hope she's well. Barcelona. My god."

I went to the closet for her coat and gloves.

"Oh Hanna, no," she said. "You can't possibly want to go for a walk in this cold."

"That's not what we're doing."

Mom and I have never confused our close relationship with being best friends. Until recent events, mine, of course, were Maura and Kelsey. Hers would be a friend from grad school who lives in L.A. and a couple of teachers at Whipple. But I knew her pretty well. Knew the moods, the soft spots, the warning signals. I picked up my coat from a chair as I said the words I knew would cheer her up.

"D'Amico's," I announced. "Crème brûlée."

7
Happy Now?

Beth had been persuasive and I had ruled in her favor: I believed Mr. Walker's mother was dead. Still, I found myself looking for Nan. Like Will said, Who was she? I cruised the 17A route a couple of times a week, slowing each time I saw an older woman waiting at a bus stop or walking on the sidewalk. Sometimes I parked and walked through the neighborhoods along the route. Like a lot of low-income areas in the city, there was plenty of life on those streets, especially as winter was at last giving up its grip. I saw lovers and dope dealers and hookers and street-corner preachers and lots of little kids from day-care centers out for walks in their miniature chain-gangs.

When I finally saw her, it almost didn't register. On one of my routine cruises through the neighborhoods along the 17A I stopped at Zip's Kwik Trip for Altoids and a lottery ticket before heading to a bookstore. The steel-plated door had slammed shut behind me, and I was almost to my car when a flash of fuchsia and red finally penetrated my musing about what I'd do with 217 million dollars. I spun on my heels and walked back into the store. The clerk looked up from a magazine and regarded my reappearance with suspicion.

Nan was by the newspaper rack. Her black pea coat hung open, revealing a wedge of bright sweater. She was talking with her jolly friend in the red coat. I took a breath and plunged in.

"Excuse me, ladies," I said in an unnaturally cheerful voice.

"Huh," Nan muttered and backed up. "You." The harsh whisper didn't seem like an opening for conversation, so I focused my charm on her friend.

Red Coat said, "We've got no money, sweetheart, so leave us alone. Go to St. Stephens, they'll feed you." She took a second look. "You seem familiar." She snapped her fingers. "That's it—the union hall. The congressman's meeting. You were in the lobby."

Nan said to me, "Do you go to a lot of his meetings?" Her voice was pure ice.

No more than you, I thought. "The Sierra Club always sends volunteers. I like to help."

She pressed her lips together tightly, not buying it.

"What do you want, dear?" asked Red Coat.

What did I want, other than to give something to Will and his family that I couldn't have? Think fast, Hanna. While they waited, I nervously looked around the grimy store and spotted a tiny section of school supplies: tablets, crayons, pencils.

"I'm an art student," I said slowly. Good, I had their attention. Now, how far could I go before the lies got too deep? "I have an assignment to do portraits of people at different stages of life. I'd love to draw your portraits."

"And what stage do you suppose she thinks we're at?" Red Coat joked to her friend.

"An interesting one," I said. I smiled at each in turn, careful to not look at Nan for too long.

She had no hesitation about staring at me. I wondered if she always wore the same suspicious gaze. I plowed ahead, still in high-gear perky. "If you had the time, we could go to the coffee shop down the block."

"Why are you really doing this?" Nan said. She had a gravelly smoker's voice.

"I really am doing it for school." I quickly calculated the money in my wallet. "Ten bucks an hour each, cash."

They liked that. Even Nan relaxed. Red Coat said, "They have good soup at that place."

"And I'll buy you lunch."

⇥⇤

Red Coat only wanted to give me their first names. "I'm Sue," she said. "And that's Nan."

"Short for Nancy?" I asked as I opened the pack of unlined white paper I'd bought at Zip's.

"No," she said. If it was shortened from some other name, she obviously wasn't going to say.

I'd intended to do separate portraits but quickly changed my mind when they sat down together. They protested slightly as I rearranged their positions and added objects to the table. When I was finally satisfied with the scene, I sat at an adjacent table and started drawing.

I made several false starts. After a good twenty minutes of producing crap, I tossed a pencil across the café at an empty chair. It bounced on the eraser and hit the wall, making a dark jagged mark on the beige surface.

"Well," said Nan, "I guess the creative juices aren't flowing today."

No sense in stooping to respond to someone's snide remark, I told myself as I reached for the box of crayons. The lid balked and I ripped it off angrily, managing to give myself a paper cut and spill the crayons at the same time.

Nan chuckled.

I glanced up and saw Sue patting her friend's hand as she murmured a soft shush. Nan rolled her eyes, then they both smiled, obviously enchanted with each other.

Holy cow, I thought. I picked up another pencil and started drawing.

We were there for two hours. I didn't think about what it would cost me.

What can I say—the drawing was terrific. Both ladies were impressed. Sue was especially pleased. "Honey, I love how you slimmed me down just a bit. Don't I wish."

"Don't wish that, Sue," Nan said. "You're lovely as is."

"Would you each like a copy?" I said to them. "I have a really good scanner and printer and you'll be pleased, I think. I can drop them off. Your families—"

"I live alone," Nan said. Her voice had lost the tender note she'd had when talking to Sue. She put on her coat. "I don't care how good a copy it is, I don't want it. I have to get downtown to the dentist. Are you paying up?" She held out her hand.

I gave her twenty dollars and she left.

Sue was still working on her chocolate cake. "Nan's a grouch sometimes," she said, "but she's mostly a dear old gal. My kids think she's a bad influence, but I don't care.

I'd love a copy of the drawing, hon. Let me give you my address and phone. Call before you come." She scribbled it on a blank sheet of paper. "Bring one for Nan too, even if she says she doesn't want it. She lives in the building one over from mine. We're back and forth all the time and I'll make sure she gets it. She has a niece who checks on both of us pretty often. I know she'd love to have it, even if Nan doesn't." Sue pushed back from the table and picked up her cane. "Now, if we're done here, I could use a ride home. And let's not forget the money."

>-<

A week later I delivered the drawings to Sue. She lived alone in a small apartment a few blocks from the store where we'd met. I wasn't surprised that the walls of her cozy living room were painted red. I *was* surprised to see packed floor-to-ceiling bookcases and stacks of books on every flat surface. I picked one up. "I've never read Flaubert," I said. I flipped it open. "And certainly not in French."

"I taught French language and literature at Augsburg College for twenty years. You're surprised, I can tell." She settled comfortably into a chair. "Wouldn't expect a college professor in this neighborhood, right? Well, it's full of people like me. Lots of us here have seen tough times and made bad choices."

"Does Nan fit into that?"

She fingered a strand of beads as she eyed me. "Do you mean has she made her own bad choices, or is she *my* bad choice? Either way, I'd rather not say." She put fingers to her lips and inhaled on a phantom cigarette. "She sure didn't like you. Nan's always a bit chilly to strangers, but oh my." She faked a shiver. "She was very cool that day. I asked her about it later. She said she didn't trust you." She pointed to the portfolio I'd set down by the couch. "Got one for her too?"

I nodded. "I could drop it off at her place."

"She's at the chiropractor until four. Every Tuesday she gets twisted and cracked. Never tried it myself. Anyway, she's not interested in a visit, she made that clear to me when I told her you'd be stopping by. And you don't cross Nan Pickard, I've learned that much. You can leave it here."

Since I hadn't expected to be invited to Nan's, I considered the information Sue had divulged a victory. Now I knew enough to track her down. Sue said, "Let's take a look at the final product. I hope you didn't turn it into something pornographic." She laughed heartily as I opened the portfolio. "Oh, my goodness," she said as I pulled out the drawing and peeled back the bubble wrap, "you didn't have to frame it."

"It was no big deal. I like making frames."

I held it before her and she inhaled sharply. "That's not the drawing you did in the coffee shop."

"I went home and started over on good paper."

"Oil pastels?"

I nodded. "This one. I used colored pencils for the other. You can pick which one you'd rather have."

Sue studied it for a very long time. "Are you in school over at MCAD? You don't look like one of those arty students, not with your khakis and pretty blue cardigan."

The Minneapolis College of Art and Design was just a few blocks away. I shook my head. "I'm a senior at Humphrey High." More or less.

"Why did you come slumming over here to find your subjects?"

"Happy accident. I was on my way somewhere."

"And you stopped at Zip's? Not many outsiders are that brave."

"The neighborhood doesn't scare me. I've taken lots of evening and summer classes at MCAD and I know the area. Besides, I needed Altoids."

She thought that was funny. "You're a very good artist, hon, but then I'm sure you know it. Let's see the other one now."

I unwrapped the second frame. She glanced between the two drawings a few times. "Was she really looking at me that way?"

I nodded. "Very affectionate."

"Huh," Sue said. "Let's give her the one in pastels. She won't admit it, but she's going to love it." She wiggled forward in her chair, grabbed her cane, and pushed up. "Let's go."

"Go where?"

"Her place. Let's not give her a chance to say she doesn't want this. We'll go hang it up for her while she's gone. You might not expect it, but she's really very sentimental. She'll like sitting in her chair and looking at the two of us. I know just the spot for it."

I smoothed the wrap down. "If she doesn't trust me, I'd better not go."

"Well, I can't carry it over, much less hang it up, not with this." She stamped the floor with her cane. "We'll do mine first. There's a hammer and some nails in the kitchen. Bottom drawer, left of the sink."

>‹

Nan's apartment was painted sage green and was filled with plants in beautiful hand-thrown pots. I lightly touched one with a black-on-black glaze and design. I pictured Nan's large, rather gnarled hands. "These are wonderful. Is she the potter?"

Sue nodded and looked sad. "She hasn't thrown a pot in years, though. The arthritis in her hands is too bad. Sometimes I think that's why she's such a grouch, not being able to do what she loves. I can't say for sure, though, because I've only known her two years. Maybe she was always that way." She checked her watch. "Let's get this up quick, then you'd better go."

We hung it on a wall adjacent to a window. "Perfect spot," I said, stepping back across the small room.

"Yes, it is. She can see it from her chair, but it's not in her face. While you're here, would you mind moving that hibiscus a bit closer to the window? It looks like it's not getting enough sun."

She aimed the cane at a plant behind me. As I turned, I noticed several black-and-white photos scattered on a small table next to a leather recliner.

One stopped me cold. "Holy cow," I murmured as I picked it up.

"Put it back," Sue said sharply.

"This is so weird. That's got to be— Ow."

Sue batted my leg with her cane as she yanked the picture from my hand. "It's time you go."

As soon as I got home, I e-mailed Will about the photo, and as soon as I sent the message, I realized it must have been completely incoherent. I'd been in a crazed rush from the moment Sue hustled me out of the apartment. I calmed myself with one of Mom's favorite acting class breathing exercises, then sent a follow-up message: *Sorry about that last e-mail. I'm not quite as nuts as it sounded. I think. Anyway, you have got to see the picture and tell me I'm not crazy. Please don't talk to anyone about this.*

I didn't hear from him for two days, which didn't help my state of mind. He finally sent a long rambling message that was partly an apology for not checking his e-mail while he was visiting his dad in D.C., partly a dangerously affectionate assurance that I wasn't crazy, and—mostly—a long description of that day's baseball practice. Guys.

I wrote back immediately: *Thanks for not thinking I'm nuts, and congrats on that batting average. Here's my idea . . .*

The following Tuesday no one answered at his house when I knocked on the kitchen door at three thirty. I pounded harder. I was just about to turn and walk to my car to wait when the door opened.

Late afternoon and Aerin was in pajamas. "Did I wake you up?" I said. "Sorry. I'm supposed to meet Will."

"I've been up. I was on the phone. He's not here."

"So, you're back," I said.

"So, my front," she replied and waved me into the house.

She still hadn't gotten a haircut, but she seemed happy and well, if you ignored the dumb joke and the pajamas late in the day. "I was just about to have breakfast," she said. "My internal clock is all screwed up."

The dishwasher hummed, a muted countertop TV showed C-SPAN, a radio played jazz. "You're not very tan for having just spent six weeks in Arizona," I said as I sat at the table.

She picked up an orange, bit into it to make a cut in the rind, and started peeling. "Those genes missed me. Will got them, though. The boy is absolutely gorgeous in summer. Hey, he's fifteen now, you know."

"I didn't know. It doesn't matter, though, because he's still too young."

"Except when you need a buddy, I guess. What are you two up to? Something to do with the mystery grandmother?"

I stared without flinching. After a short dose of that, she laughed and offered me an orange section. "Your mother could do that too. She had this look that would quiet the class in no time. Made her seem about six feet tall."

"I've seen it often."

She separated the rest of the orange and set the pieces out in a neat row on a napkin. "I could use a buddy too. Want to go dancing again some time?"

"Love to. Tell me when."

"Some weekend. I'm babysitting the boy. Mom's in New York this month, and Dad—" She pointed at the TV. "Whaddya know: There he is now."

C-SPAN's cameras had returned to covering the slow action in Congress. A group of men and women huddled between desks. Aerin's dad said something to the others, making them laugh. His own laugh settled into a smile. My breath escaped in a long sigh. I wasn't crazy.

Aerin put an orange section into her mouth. "It's still kind of a trip seeing him on camera like that." She wiped a dribble of juice off her chin. "Babysitting's not the only reason I came home. I've got some work. Another jingle, this time for a car dealer. Don't say a thing, Hanna. Not a blessed thing, okay?"

I didn't say a thing.

"And I guess I can only vegetate and be blue for so long at a time. I think that's probably a sign of mental health, don't you? Would you eat some eggs if I scrambled a bunch?"

I checked my watch. If Will took too long, we'd miss Nan's return from the chiropractor and would either have to wait another week or just sit and watch for her and get lucky. True, we could ring apartment buzzers until someone let us inside the building, which likely we'd have to do anyway, because I was beginning to doubt if accosting her on the sidewalk was the right way—

"Hanna? Eggs? C'mon, it shouldn't that big a decision."

I brought myself back to the kitchen. "Yes, please. Thank you."

We'd just finished eating when Will burst in. "You're finally up?" he said to Aerin. He turned to me. "She's been sleeping nonstop for about two days. We should go. Sorry I'm late. Our first game is Friday and the coach was pissed about me taking off and he reamed me out for a long time." He turned back to Aerin. "If by any chance he calls, back me up on Grandpa being in the hospital, okay?"

"Actually he's home putting up a new birdfeeder he built. I just talked to Grandma."

"I had to give a good excuse. Please back me up."

"How can you have a game when there's still snow on the ground?" I said.

"The field's been cleared. Let's go."

"Slow down," Aerin said. "I need to get dressed."

Will and I looked at each other. "You aren't invited," he said to her. "And you aren't welcome."

"Don't care. Until Dad gets home Thursday night I'm in charge of you, so I don't need to be invited. The way I figure it, you two either need a chaperone, in which case I should go along, or you don't need a chaperone but are doing something interesting, in which case I should go along." She looked at us as we looked at each other. "And I'm guessing it's something interesting." When we didn't answer, she said, "I'll be ready in two minutes."

><

Aerin ripped open the small bag of potato chips she'd brought from home. "I've never been on a stakeout before. You kids do such fun things on your dates."

"Shut up," Will said wearily.

"You know Mom hates it when we say that."

I slumped behind the wheel. "Why is it that every time I'm with more than one Walker child, I feel lucky not to have siblings?" Before they could think up a suitable retort, I straightened. "There she is, getting off the bus." Will started to get out, but I grabbed his arm. "Let her go."

Aerin said, "That's the woman who has a picture of our dad? I was hoping for someone a little more glamorous. Dang, these chips are stale."

"Hanna," said Will, "why are we here if we're not going to talk to her? She's practically inside the building now. How will we get in if the door's locked?"

"She's a suspicious and touchy woman, Will. I think

the only way she might ever talk is if she's not out in public."

Nan disappeared. The only sound in the car was the crunching of potato chips.

After a few minutes Will sighed. "Are we going or aren't we?"

"I don't know what to do," I said. "Suddenly this seems like a horrible intrusion."

Aerin mashed up the chip bag and opened the car door. "Of course it is, but why should that stop us? I bet she's inside her apartment by now. Let's surprise her before she's too settled." She stepped out into a slushy snowbank and made a face. "I've got to live somewhere there's no snow and they have good mass transit. Move it, you two."

We slipped into the building as someone came out. An Out of Order sign was taped to the elevator. Aerin led the way up the stairs.

Nan's place was at the end of a dark hallway. Televisions played loudly in every apartment we passed. We stood in front of her door. Apparently it was up to me to make the move. I raised my hand to knock, then dropped it. "I'm having second thoughts."

"Not me," said Aerin. "I'm having a good time." She pounded on the door.

There was no sound from inside the apartment, but after a moment I could detect movement behind the peephole. Locks clicked and a chain dropped. The door swung open. Nan looked at Will and Aerin before fixing her furious stare on me. "Sierra Club," she hissed. "I knew you were lying about that." She walked back into the apartment, leaving the door open. She sat down in the leather chair and glared at us. "Don't stand there like dopes; the cat will get out."

Aerin strode in; Will and I followed slowly. I glanced toward the table by her chair. All of the photos were gone. I looked toward the window. My drawing had also disappeared.

Nan reached for a pack of Kools and tapped one out. "Sue told me about the other day, so I know why you've come." She lit the cigarette and looked at Will and Aerin. "With them in tow, to boot." She pointed her lighter at Aerin. "I've never seen you at your daddy's meetings, but I know who you are. You're the one who had the car crash."

Will stiffened and caught his breath. I took his hand.

"Gotta be tough, losing someone that way. And three of them—whew!"

"Yes," Aerin said.

"Were they good friends, or just people you worked with?"

"They were my best friends."

"Lovers?"

"No."

Nan hooted softly. "All that time on the road and no tumbling into each other's arms? I find that hard to believe."

"They were my friends." Aerin's voice had weakened. She unzipped her jacket and sat on the green couch.

"Feel free to sit down," Nan said, "but I hope you don't expect refreshments."

Aerin opened her mouth, then it froze in a slight *O*. I followed her gaze.

The drawing I'd done of Nan and Sue was on the floor under the table by Nan's chair. The glass over the drawing was cracked. Had it fallen, or had it been used as a target?

Aerin leaned forward. "Hanna thinks you have a picture of our father and that you might know something about our grandmother," she said. "But I guess I don't really want to use that word for her. How about we call her the woman who took off one day while her son was at kindergarten and who let him come home to an empty apartment."

Nan looked at me. "But you were stalking me before you ever saw the photo. Huh. I knew you were lying about needing to do our portraits."

I nodded. "I lied. I was curious. I'd heard you and Sue talking after the meeting at the union hall. Then you showed up at the community center and when you saw their sister, you were so upset. I figured there had to be a reason. I guessed you were their missing grandmother, but now I don't think you are."

"Huh," she said again. She closed her eyes and took a long drag. As she exhaled, a smile appeared. She was savoring something.

The air was thick with smoke and tension. No one said a thing while she finished the cigarette. The cat appeared and wove around all eight legs before jumping onto Aerin and settling in.

Nan dropped the smoldering Kool into a pop can. She leaned back, hands behind her head. "I'm certainly not their grandmother." She glanced at Aerin. "Or whatever you condescend to call her. As for me, most of the time I called her Angel." She chuckled, watching us react. "That's right. I knew her."

Will sat with his sister and me on the sofa while we listened to the story.

"I wasn't the love of her life," Nan said thoughtfully, staring at some distant point. "She went both ways and played too hard with everyone to ever lose her heart to one man or woman. But she was the love of mine, oh my god yes. We met in Seattle at a bar she worked at. When she found out I was from Minneapolis, she nearly threw me out of the place on the spot for no other reason than that. She didn't have fond memories of the city, to put it mildly. She calmed down quickly, that was always her way. I stayed in Seattle five years just to be with her. Then she left without a word. That was her way too. We had another short time together a few years later when I tracked her down in Nashville. It didn't last. Jill was always leaving. She always—"

"Jill?" Aerin blurted.

For some reason Nan ignored her and spoke to Will. "Naomi Walker wasn't her real name. Hell, you kids had better go. I'm getting tired. I usually nap after I go to the chiro."

"What was her real name?" Aerin asked.

Nan shook her head, still directing her attention to Will. "It was Jill. You don't need the last name because I won't have you tracking down all the pieces of her story like you tracked me down. Don't you get it? She didn't want your father in her life, and that means all of you too. But she knew about him," she snapped, finally looking at Aerin. "She knew that he grew up just fine and she knew about all you kids. She had no regrets about what she did.

He must not either—look how it paid off for him. He's never hesitated to brag in his campaigns or to reporters about how he overcame his tough little-abandoned-boy childhood."

"My father never brags," Aerin said sharply, "and he hates to talk about his childhood."

Nan shrugged. "So you say, but there's been plenty about all that in the papers and magazines over the years, especially when he had an election to win or some issue to push. That's how Jill found out about him, from a magazine story. It wasn't like she went looking. Still, every now and then when he was on the national news she'd call me long distance from wherever she was and tell me to watch."

"Why did she run out on him?" Will asked angrily.

"She didn't like being a mother. She didn't like herself when she was a mother."

"Why not?" Aerin said. "Did she hit him? Or do worse, maybe?"

Nan stared at her coldly. "She knew he'd be better off without her." She cleared her throat. "Jill had no regrets, but she carried plenty of guilt, if that makes you feel any better. I think it's why she never—" She sighed and looked down at her hands, muttering under her breath.

"Never what?" I asked.

Nan turned her stare on me. "Jill knew she'd cheated her little boy out of a normal life. I'm pretty sure that's why she never let herself be happy in love and settle down."

"Settle down with you, you mean," Aerin said. "So now

you're mad at our father because he has a family? You resent him for being happy?"

"If I resent anything," Nan snapped, "it's this intrusion of my privacy."

Aerin stiffened and folded her hands in her lap.

"Your father grew up fine and Jill died all alone," Nan continued. "Some would say that's justice."

Her shoulders suddenly heaved and she coughed violently into her hand. "I moved back to Minneapolis three years ago to be closer to my sister and her kids. I started seeing your dad on the news and in the paper and it made me miss her so bad all over again. I tell you, when her neighbor called me from Toledo five years ago to say she'd died, it almost cracked me open."

"*Five* years ago?" Will said.

"Now I know we're not talking about the right woman," said Aerin. "Our dad found out long ago that she was dead."

"I don't doubt that 'Naomi Walker' died a long time ago," Nan said, "but I have no idea who the hell she was. Jill stopped using that name the day she left Minneapolis and left your father." She coughed again. "Want to know how she came up with it? 'Naomi' was just something she spotted in a magazine and liked for a while. Walker? Well, she told me once that your dad was conceived in a railroad hotel in Walker, Minnesota. Don't ask me who the father was. I'm pretty certain she didn't know."

Aerin stood. "You've got a mean spirit, Ms. Pickard. I don't believe any of it. Let's go, guys."

Nan picked up a small book from the table next to her chair. It was bound in fake leather and had gold lettering on the cover: *Page A Day*. The diary was stuffed with letters, newspaper clippings, and photos She pulled out a black-and-white picture. "This is what you came for. Go ahead and take a look. It was taken years before I knew her." Both Aerin and Will reached for the picture. Nan pulled it away from them as she turned to me. "Why didn't you bring the other sister? I shouldn't have run that day at the center, but I got too upset. It was Jill's birthday, see, and then *she* appeared in the door out of nowhere and it was such a shock. Spitting image of Jill." She closed her eyes and, smiling, drifted away someplace.

She didn't resist when I slipped the photo from her fingers and handed it to Will and Aerin. "Oh, my god," Aerin whispered. "Hanna, you're right."

"Weird," Will said.

The photo showed a young woman in front of a Christmas tree. She was staring at a little boy. He wore pajamas and a cowboy hat and smiled broadly for the camera.

I tapped the picture. "She's what really blew me away. I mean, I hardly know Beth, but that's her exactly: incredibly pretty and a don't-mess-with-me attitude."

Nan chuckled. "Oh, Sierra Club, too funny; that's just how Jill was. In case your friends still have doubts, check the back of the picture."

Aerin turned it over. *Naomi and Mark, Xmas 1953.* Someone had drawn a line through *Naomi* and written *Jill* above it.

"I don't know who took the picture," Nan said. "It was in a box of stuff her neighbor sent me after she died. I fixed the name."

Will said, "Ma'am, you've got to let us borrow this

photo. We'll make a copy and bring it back. We've never seen a picture of our dad as a kid. He probably never has. You've got to."

"Don't got to." She wiggled her fingers. "Give it back now. It's the only one I have of her. She hated cameras." She leaned forward. "C'mon."

"Please?" Aerin asked.

"Grab it, would you?" Nan said to me. "Then get them out of here."

Will's eyes pleaded as I eased the picture from his fingers. "It's hers," I whispered.

Nan yanked it out of my hand. Will swore and turned toward the door.

Aerin said, "How did she die? She couldn't have been very old."

"Well, I'll tell you this: She wasn't lucky enough to go quick"—Nan snapped her fingers—"in a car crash. Tell me—is it true that the other girl in the band was decapitated?"

"How did she die?" Aerin asked again, her voice suddenly as fragile and cool as frost. "Our father will want to know that much."

They were locked in some sort of silent battle. Finally Nan said, "Once upon a time some man tried to mess with her in a bar. Too many men think that any woman who works in a bar is always happy to serve up more than drinks. Jill defended herself from that particular SOB with her nail file. He got thirteen stitches and was sent home from the ER to his nice house and wife. She got five months in a Tennessee county lock-up. Second week inside, her appendix blew. Prison's no place to be when you need medical care. They gave her bad blood during surgery and the rest of her life she had hepatitis. That's what killed her. Her liver finally gave out five years ago." Nan shook her head as she swore softly. "She defends herself against some thug and gets prison and a slow death sentence. You crash a car and kill three people and walk around free as you please."

"You bitch!" Will shouted. He lunged toward her.

Aerin and I grabbed him at the same time. When he had stilled, Aerin took him by the arm and left the apartment. I followed, turning to look at Nan as I pulled the door closed.

She smiled and said, "Happy now?"

⇥⇤

Aerin and Will were on the landing below. His eyes were closed and he was muttering. She was leaning against the wall. Suddenly she straightened and slammed the heel of her palm against his shoulder. "If Beth and I have tried to get *anything* straight in your boy brain, it's that you *never* call a girl or a woman a bitch."

"Jesus, Aerin," he whispered. "She's nuts. Crazy and mean."

She made a noise, then fell against him and buried her face in his jacket. Will wrapped his arms around his sister. Her breath came in sharp gasps. "Oh, god, why doesn't it ever stop? I didn't kill them, Will. I did not kill them. Why do people say that? I didn't. I miss them so much."

I slipped past them. I got to the next landing and dropped to a step.

Aerin's sobs and Will's soothing murmurs echoed in the bare stairwell.

I closed my eyes and leaned my head against the cinderblock wall. Nothing to do but wait. I'd done too much already.

>‹<

I wasn't surprised when they asked me to drop them off at their grandparents'. It was a quiet trip. Aerin sat alone in the back, staring somberly out the window. Will sat unbuckled next to me, half-turned in his seat, keeping an eye on his sister.

After a few minutes she said, "Buckle up, Will." It was the only thing anyone said the entire trip.

Their grandparents were standing in the front yard, looking at the bare ground near the house. They turned around and waved when I parked. "Grandma said she'd spotted some crocuses," Aerin said. "That's probably what they're looking at. Would you like to meet them, Hanna?"

I shook my head. "I need to go home and I need to get out of your lives. I am so sorry about what happened. I should have talked to her first before I dragged you two into it."

"That's ridiculous," Aerin said as she opened the car door.

"It's all my fault," Will said glumly.

"Oh, great," Aerin said. "Now we're all feeling like crap." She slammed the car door, then motioned me to open my window. It whirred down. "Hanna, we saw a picture of our dad as a kid. Do you have any idea how cool that is? Seeing that outfit he had on was worth a little breakdown." She managed a smile. "What a strange scene that was. What do you say I go find a piano and you find a pencil and then we each try to make sense of what happened?"

"My stupid drawings are what started this whole disaster. I should never have—"

She once again placed a finger on my lips to shush me. "Your drawing of those two women was almost more interesting than the photo of Dad. I wish I could have gotten a better look. What I saw blew me away. Nan looked so happy in it. Hard to believe, right? At first I couldn't understand why you'd done it that way, because she seems so bitter. I was dying to pick up the picture and figure it out. Then as she was talking, I got it. Simple, really: She's in love with that lady. Once upon a time I bet she stared at my grandmother with the same expression. What a story, Hanna Martin. Makes me want to write a song." She glanced over at her brother. "Please get out, Will. I need you to get out and say good-bye. It's exhausting chaperoning you two. Hanna, I have a feeling now that I probably won't be staying in Minneapolis for too long, so it might be a while before we go dancing. Whaddya say we promise each other not to wallow." She pressed the back of her hand against my cheek, then turned and walked across the snow toward her grandparents.

Will opened his car door. "I didn't see the drawing."

"It was kind of hidden."

"I wish I'd seen it. And I wish Mom and Dad could see that photo. We've got to get it from her, Hanna. She doesn't deserve to have it. Will you help me get it? She'd talk to you."

"No, Will. I'm not going back and neither are you. The photo is hers."

"I wish Beth could see it. She really does look like that woman. It was weird." He closed the car door. "I don't believe all of that actually happened. She was so mean to Aerin. Why? It was like she especially wanted to hurt her. I can't believe how mad I got. I've *never* felt like that before. Why did she say those things to Aerin?"

"I don't know. Maybe because the love of her life is dead and Aerin somehow escaped dying. Maybe because she's sick and unhappy and she wanted to make someone else feel bad too. Maybe she guessed it would be easy to hurt Aerin. I don't know."

"That photo," he said softly. "It's the only one we've ever seen of him when he was little." His head jerked up. "Hey, maybe you could draw a copy, Hanna."

"I don't think so. I didn't look at it long enough. Will, I'll do this: I need to apologize to both Nan and her friend. I'll write them and I'll plant the idea with her friend about getting a copy of the picture. Who knows, maybe someday Nan will change her mind."

He nodded. "I guess." Then he pointed. "I'm so scared for her, Hanna." We both looked across the yard to where Aerin had fallen into her grandmother's arms. "She's so beat up," Will whispered, "and now she says she's taking off again. I hate it when she gets so blue she has to run off. She's not going to make it back one of these times."

Aerin dropped her head on her grandmother's shoulder. Safe landing, I thought. "She's okay," I said.

"How can you say that? Look at her."

Aerin and her grandparents walked slowly into the house.

"When she takes off she goes to visit friends in Arizona, right?"

"Family friends. She doesn't have that many others. The band was everything to her."

"And when she's there she walks in the desert and it's quiet."

He shrugged.

"There's a piano," I said. Her North Star, I thought. Her true point through crazy dark water. "She'll make it; she knows the way back."

Will looked at me blankly. Oh, bloody hell. So perfect and so young. I squeezed his hand. "You were really sweet with her."

He crumpled at my touch. "Hanna, I wish we were together. It's crazy that we aren't. I know we could fix it. Even if our parents are freaked about the age thing or about us jumping into bed so fast, I know we could calm them down."

"Will, I have way too much to fix in my own life right now. I can't be messing up yours anymore. I've done enough. Besides, after they find out about today, your parents will absolutely hate me."

"They won't. Couldn't we just—"

"Stop it, Will. We can't do anything. I absolutely need some space from all of this and all of you Walkers. I don't want you to call me or e-mail me and . . ." My voice weakened. "And I definitely don't want you to drop by the house and sit in my kitchen."

"I want to be with you again," he whispered. "I think about that so much."

I took his face in my hands and kissed him once more. "Good-bye, Will."

>←

Several news vans and a few emergency vehicles were parked by Lake Calhoun when I drove home on the parkway. I spotted a crowd near the shoreline and then looked away, keeping my eyes fixed on the road. I refused to look a second time. "I can't handle another thing," I said as I turned off the parkway. "Not another thing today."

Whipple's spring show opened in one week, and Mom was embroiled in final rehearsals and wouldn't be home for hours. I sat in the kitchen, trying not to see the scene in Nan's apartment or the image of Aerin's collapse, but they looped again and again in my head. I fought it for almost three minutes before I slipped back into my shoes and went out for a walk.

The crowd at the lake had grown. I joined the gawkers. A tow truck and police car were parked at the water's edge. I tapped a woman on the shoulder. "What's going on? Did some fool try swimming now that the ice is out?"

"They're finally towing out that ATV from last winter's crash. It was too dangerous for the divers to do it when there was still ice. Oh my, are you all right, dear?"

I hurried away, making it only as far as the playground before I dropped onto a bench. "Not today," I said. "Why today?"

A runner did a double take as she passed me. She reversed direction and ran back. She jogged in place in front of the bench. "Are you all right?" I nodded and lifted a hand to wave her off. She glanced over her shoulder twice as she ran down the path.

The ATV emerged slowly from the dark water. The

tow chain pulled it forward in jerks until it was all the way up on the bed of the truck. The crowd watched in horrified fascination.

I plunged my hands deep into my coat pockets. My right hand jammed hard against my phone. I pulled it out and held it tightly.

A TV cameraman trolled for reaction shots in the crowd. The reporter with him spotted me. Like the two women I'd worried, she saw something going on in my expression. The others had been concerned; she smelled a story.

Get up and go, I ordered myself as she approached with a hungry smile on her face. My legs wouldn't move. I pulled off my mittens and defended myself the only way I could: I got busy on the phone, dialing the first number that popped into my head.

As soon as Kelsey answered, I started talking. "It's Hanna. I know it's been a while, but today has been suck-city and I think I may explode. I'm down at the Calhoun playground. You would not believe . . ." The reporter made a face and made some impatient noises while I talked. When it became obvious I wasn't getting off the phone, she turned and walked back to the crowd. My breath snagged. "Sorry, Kels; I'll call again later," I said, abruptly ending the call.

Once the tow truck pulled away, the crowd quickly thinned. The reporters went back to their vans. The people who remained all milled around two couples who were accepting hugs from everyone.

The parents.

No one seemed in a hurry to leave. Oddly, people were

smiling; some even laughed. Closure, I thought. So that's what it looks like.

It took a while, but finally only a few people remained with the two couples. I hauled myself up off the bench and walked toward them.

I must have looked grim as hell. Conversations stopped when I approached.

One of the mothers spotted me. She said something to the others and moved in my direction.

What did I think I was doing? I looked around for an escape. A red car sped into view up on the parkway. It pulled over into a parking bay.

"Hello," the woman said. "I don't think we've met. Did you know the kids? I'm Mercy Johnston, Derek's mom."

I shook my head. "I didn't know them. Derek was a friend of a friend. They played hockey together. I just wanted to say I'm sorry." I glanced up again just as Maura and Kelsey—ignoring the stairway a few yards to their right—tried standing and sliding down the thin crust of icy snow on the slope from the street. They fell within seconds and tumbled, shrieking and laughing the rest of the way.

I bit back a smile. Derek's mom looked puzzled. I took a deep breath. "Mrs. Johnston, I saw them that night. Derek and Lindsey, I mean. I'd taken a walk and was sitting on a bench and they stopped to visit before they went out on the ice. Then I went home. I guess maybe I was the last person who saw them."

"Oh, my goodness," she murmured.

"It was such a beautiful night to be out. They were

having a good time. The moment I saw them, I knew they were happy."

"Thank you," she whispered.

I smiled, touched her shoulder, and walked toward my friends.

><

After they rescued me from the scene at the lake, Maura and Kelsey took me home. We spent the evening making up and catching up.

I held back nothing. They heard about Aerin's scars, her meltdown in the stairwell, Sue's cluttered red apartment, Will's apparent preference for knit boxers, and his mother's icy blue eyes. I showed them every drawing I'd done over the winter and the three surviving photos of Lydia Cortland.

They talked too. I heard about Maura's blow-up with Brian, Kelsey's confession to Zak, his "Have a nice life" reaction, Spencer's new girlfriend in Ann Arbor, Maura's full-ride scholarship to NYU, and Kelsey's perfect record of five Ivy League "Yes" letters.

Anger was there on all sides when we started, but without any one of us noticing exactly when, it was swept off, carried along by the rush and force of a conversation pent up for too long. When we were finally exhausted from talking, we moved to the kitchen to find something to eat.

"By the way," Maura said to me as she made a peanut butter sandwich, "I forgive you."

"*You* forgive *me*?"

"Here we go," Kelsey said as she looked into the fridge. She sighed loudly. "It's going to start all over."

Maura licked the peanut butter from the knife. She nodded. "For freezing us out and choosing to let a bad thing get worse. I accept responsibility for the bad part, but you . . ." She shook her head.

When I didn't speak, Kelsey sighed again. "Don't you think," she said, "that the idea of forgiveness is kind of religious? And you know, I've never really liked that part of religion. How old is this piece of cheesecake?" She removed a clear plastic take-out box from the back of the refrigerator, opened it, and made a face before putting it on the counter. "Old enough to kill."

Before Maura and I could hammer out the details of forgiveness, Mom arrived. As soon as she saw the three of us in the kitchen, delight vanquished her end-of-day exhaustion. She didn't say anything about them being there for the first time in months, but she did give each of them a hard hug before wondering aloud about finding something to eat.

"There's peanut butter," Maura said. "I'll make you a sandwich."

"And cheesecake," added Kelsey, pointing, "but I'd be careful with that."

As the three of them looked at the moldy dessert and laughed, I framed the scene, rearranging things in my head and debating how to capture it. Pastels? Colored pencils? My fingers tapped. Oils, maybe. And I could use that good birch board I had stashed in the closet. I worked it over in my head, not quite seeing the picture yet, not quite sure what I'd use to catch the color and light and mood, but I was absolutely clear on the meaning of the scene: lighthouse.

"What is going on in your brain?" Maura blurted.

I looked at her with unfocused eyes. "Safe landing," I whispered.

"What?"

I took a breath and reentered the kitchen. "Just thinking I might send you home so I could go work."

"That's great," said Kelsey. "You don't talk to us for weeks and then you kick us out to go draw."

"Paint," I murmured.

Mom said, "Obviously it's time for me to go take a hot shower and let you three work this out."

"Not so fast, Claudia," said Maura. "We need to catch up with you too. Tell me: Are you and the boyfriend talking about marriage yet?"

Mom froze in the doorway.

Kelsey's soft chuckle released the pause button and we all breathed and moved.

Mom said, "A little bit, yes."

"Keep us posted," Maura replied. Mom made her escape, shaking her head. After she'd disappeared and we heard her footsteps upstairs, Maura turned to me. "Wedding bells soon?"

"I don't think so. I don't really know. That's the first I've heard about it. Wow. I would never have asked her that."

"I know, Hanna," Maura said. "Why do you think I did?"

Kelsey added, "That's why you need your friends."

⇥⇤

Grad parties are a weird social institution, ranking right up there with weddings as a blatant way to hold out your hand and ask for gifts. Around here the usual thing to do is host an open house for a couple of hours on a weekend day close to the big event. You provide food, keep a smile on your face, and try not to be too obvious about looking at the cards and gifts as they pile up. Because there are always several parties scheduled at the same time, friends make hit-and-run appearances while the adults hang around forever.

As June grew closer I'd resisted even discussing the subject of the party. When Mom finally cornered me and threw her weight around, I really resisted. I hated the thought of being the center of attention.

Mom resisted my resistance, pulling on a stony talk-all-you-want-but-it-makes-no-difference expression when I argued my side. She clinched it by playing the guilt card.

"You can't really expect your grandparents to drag their spouses halfway across the country and not have some celebration besides sitting on bleachers in a huge arena waiting for the ten seconds you cross the stage. They should meet your friends and mine. We're having the party."

We sent the invitations and we had the party.

It was on a beautiful blue-sky June day. People started coming at noon on the dot. Three hours later—a full hour past the official end time—there was still a respectable crowd, both inside the house (where I reigned) and in the back and front yards (where Mom spent most of the afternoon shamelessly soliciting and accepting compliments on her garden).

Maura and Kelsey had hung around the whole time; we had plans to go together to more parties later. The other lingerers were all neighbors and Mom's friends, plus a few old colleagues of Dad's who'd come to say hello to my grandmother. I decided I had no obligation to stay any longer.

"Jeez, I'd forgotten how cool your grandfather is," Maura said as soon as we were in her car. "I didn't know he'd been to Antarctica."

"He was only there to check out the possibility of ruining it by drilling for oil, so don't be too charmed."

Mom and some neighbors were standing on the front steps greeting the letter carrier. Mom held a nearly-empty tray of champagne glasses and she offered one to him. He hesitated, looked around, then shrugged and took a glass as he handed her our mail.

She glanced down at the bundle, looked up to smile at something someone said, and then did a very bad sitcom double take. She stared at the mail a long time before looking up and spotting me. With effort, she smiled. Just as Maura pulled away from the curb, Mom dropped the mail on the tray and blew me a kiss.

"Hold it," I barked. "I've got to get out. I'll be right back."

Mom excused herself from the group and tried to make a break for the house. She's nimble, but my legs are longer. I caught up just as she put a hand on the door. "Oh, Hanna," she said. "Go to your parties. It can wait."

"I used to think you were a good actor. Let me see it." Inside the house, my grandfather's booming laugh sparked more loud laughter. Mom turned away from the door. With a deep sigh, she lifted the tray and served me the mail.

I picked up the thin beige envelope. "I didn't really expect this. I honestly thought my letter would just get bounced back." I sat down and tugged on her skirt until she sat beside me. "Cool stamps," I said. I held the envelope with both hands. "Too bad I stopped collecting them. Remember how good Grandpa used to be about sending letters from all the places he went to so I'd have the stamps? I don't think he ever went to Spain, though."

She eyed the letter like it carried some toxin. Well, why not. How could it be anything but a reminder of the first time her life came to a crashing halt?

"Mom, even if by some crazy chance the letter is affectionate and apologetic, I'm so sorry I did this. It was dumb to go chasing after some ghost. It was dumb to think a phantom grandmother could fill what was missing."

She was wearing the jade and silver necklace. It had shifted, and I straightened the chain until the clasp was centered at the back of her neck. "Especially when nothing was missing."

She took my hand and kissed it, then nodded toward the letter. "Even I don't feel like avoiding the inevitable any longer. You may as well open it."

I touched the return address. "I guess she's not hiding anymore." I slit the envelope with a thumbnail and pulled out a single sheet of stationery.

Mom said, "Please read it to yourself." She looked away.

I scanned the brief message, then started over out loud.

Dear Hanna Martin,

    I apologize for the delay in responding to your kind note. I avoid Barcelona during the spring tourist season, and my mail did not catch up with me until I returned. Then, too, I'm sure you would not be surprised to hear I was uncertain as to whether I should reply at all. I deliberated for some time.

Thank you for the drawing. The simple lines and bold colors make quite a powerful combination. I confess I find myself studying it often.

I had an aunt who could paint quite well. Sadly, she let her talent languish. I hope you work hard and develop your gift.

I'm very grateful, Hanna, that you reached across the years to introduce yourself and share the news of your impending graduation and plans for college.

I wish you and your mother all the best.

> *Cordially,*
> *Lydia Cortland*

After a moment Mom cleared her throat and pointed to the street. "Maura and Kelsey want you."

I waved them on. Maura made a face and raised a hand: *What?* I waved again. The Prizm sped away.

I read the letter twice more, silently. "I can't tell at all what she's really thinking or feeling. And I can't imagine what you're feeling, Mom." I handed her the letter.

She dropped it on the tray. "I'm feeling a little concerned about our guests."

"Our guests are fine." I took the last glass of champagne. When she didn't indicate I should put it back, I sipped.

"And I'm feeling more than a little bit curious," she said softly.

"God, no lie. I bet she is too. Next move is ours, right?"

Mom shook her head. "No, I'm curious about which drawing it was that you sent her."

I sipped more champagne, then put the glass back on the tray. "I guess this stuff is an acquired taste."

She waited.

"One of the pastels I did in Hawaii last summer."

"Which one?"

"Dancer at Fifty." I slipped my arm through hers. "I sent her a picture of you."

8

What Happens Next?

I turned to the lady sitting next to me and said, "What do you think: Can the driver get the bus unstuck or will we be walking home in the snow?"

She made a scoffing noise. She shifted on the seat and pulled her shopping bag into her arms. "He'll work it out. This is nothing. These Chicago bus drivers have to deal with worse than this all the time. You must not have lived here very long."

"About three years."

The man across from us spoke up, "That explains it, then. We've had three easy winters in a row. This will be a good one; you're in for a treat."

"I grew up in Minneapolis, so I'm used to winter. You know where they can't handle it? Rhode Island. I was in school there for a year, and every time there was even a little snow, they panicked."

Another man said, "That's how it is down south too. A few flakes and they're sliding off the road."

The bus rocked and groaned before pushing forward and continuing around the corner. The people in my section of the bus cheered and clapped. I looked back and saw a demolished snowbank spread across a crosswalk.

The heater on the bus was blasting. I unzipped my coat, then dug in my backpack and pulled out the lunch I hadn't touched. The lady next to me lifted her eyebrows as I took a peanut butter sandwich out of a plastic bag. "Is that your supper, honey?"

"Lunch. I was too busy at work to eat."

The bus came to a sliding halt a few feet beyond a crowded bus stop. People filed in slowly. Their shoulders and hats were coated in soft snow.

My seatmate pointed to the work ID hanging around my neck. "Goodman Theater. Are you an actress?"

I shook my head and then washed down the sandwich with a swig of SunnyD. "I work part-time in the scene shop."

"Building things, like a carpenter?"

"Pretty much."

She poked the shoulder of the man sitting in the seat that was at right angles to ours. It was an unnecessary move because he was obviously listening. "She's a carpenter."

"It's student employment, actually," I said. "Kind of an internship. I go to DePaul."

"You're going to college to learn how to be a carpenter?" another man said, his voice sharp in disbelief.

I laughed. "That's exactly how my grandfather feels." The bus aisle was getting jammed. I saw a weary pregnant woman. I rose and signaled her over. "My stop is coming up." I pulled gloves out of a pocket and smiled at my seatmate as I stepped away.

"Oh, honey," she said. "No hat in this weather?"

"Left it on the bus last week. Safe trip, everyone." Before I'd even turned away they'd launched into a conversation about odd or precious things they'd found on buses and trains over the years.

Head down against the snow, I trudged the four blocks from the bus stop to my apartment building. As I passed a pizza joint that was popular with a lot of DePaul theater majors, I was tempted to go in. No doubt I could find friends inside who'd be ready to split a pitcher of beer and a pizza. The door opened and noise escaped. Just as I was about to turn in, a burst of wind tore down the street, blowing up snow and blinding me for a moment. "Head home, Hanna," I said. I had cold pizza in the fridge.

Inside my building I crouched to peer into my mailbox. A single envelope lay at an angle in the narrow space. The lock balked for a moment, then gave way. I pulled out the letter and laughed. Mom had overstamped again. She and Charles had been living in Toronto for how many years? She still didn't get the postage straight. I slipped the stiff envelope into my pocket, picked up a copy of the free neighborhood newspaper from the stack on the foyer floor, and started climbing to the fifth floor.

The apartment was stifling hot. The radiator hissed as I entered. I locked the door behind me, dropped my bag on a chair, and hung my coat in the small front closet. Home sweet home, I thought as I kicked off my shoes. It's Friday night, there's a raging blizzard, and I don't have to go anywhere.

Mom had sent a check and photos of their new apartment. I kissed the check and pinned it on the bulletin board, then sat down to look at the pictures. There was one of her in a bathrobe in the kitchen. She looked positively disheveled and carefree. Obviously marriage was helping her unwind. I put it under a magnet on the fridge next to a picture of Maura, Kelsey, and me in Barcelona. As I set the rest of the photos down on the counter I noticed the butter dish and groaned. Why hadn't I put it away? The lid had been knocked off and there were telltale impressions of a tongue. "Where are you hiding?" I shouted as I dumped the cat-licked butter into the garbage and put the dish into the sink. "Are you sleeping off your butter high?" I heard a muffled sleepy meow.

The pizza reheated beautifully, there was one bottle of beer left over from a weekend party, Tracy Chapman sang on the college radio station. A good night. I sat down with the pizza, spread the paper out on the table, and turned to the entertainment section. If there were any interesting CD reviews, maybe I'd get something new tomorrow.

There was a cranky but funny review of the new Madonna CD that was long enough to be a senior thesis. *Continued on B-13.* "What else is there to say about her?" I said aloud. "Why is she still recording and why am I even reading this?" I sighed. "And why am I talking to myself?" There was no answer of course, so, as usual, I provided my own. "Because you live alone with a cat, you're marooned by the blizzard, and there's no one else to talk to."

As I turned the page, my eyes landed on music listings for Hot Foot, a nearby club. Fish Bowl, an excellent local group, was headlining tonight at ten. But it was the opening act that caught my eye: Friday 8:00 P.M., Sylvia Callahan.

When I had resumed breathing I went to the window and looked out. The snowy street was deserted except for a single woman who stood in a doorway trying valiantly to light a cigarette in the wind. "Looks like a fine night for music," I said. As if she'd heard me, the woman looked up as she took a deep victorious drag on her smoke.

Two hours later, as I stood in the hall locking the door, my neighbor appeared in the stairway carrying a loaded laundry basket. "Are you nuts, Hanna? Or haven't you noticed the blizzard?"

"Going to Hot Foot," I replied. "I'm in the mood for music."

She shook her head as she opened her door. "At least put a hat on."

I went back into my apartment and into the bedroom. Roscoe was half hidden beneath the pile of pillows on the bed. I dug him out and pulled the yellow striped cap from his head. I slapped off four years of dust and tugged it down over my ears.

>‹

Hot Foot was half empty. It still wasn't quite eight o'clock, but with the weather getting worse I doubted if there'd be too many more people coming. I found a small table off to the side and settled in.

The surly waitress had just brought me a beer when

the lights dimmed. Aerin walked quickly to the microphone. She slipped on her guitar, checked the tuning, and started playing.

The first two numbers were impressive bluesy songs that got the audience interested. The third was a funny self-mocking love song that had people laughing. Then she slid into a crazy instrumental that won them over.

She'd put on weight, I decided. Still wearing her hair too long. And—though it was probably a trick of the lighting—she looked a little bit tan.

Aerin acknowledged each round of the steadily louder applause with a nod and smile. After she'd finished an intricate cover of a wry Dylan song, some drunk joker behind me shouted, "Marry me, Sylvia!" Aerin glanced up, squinted a bit in the lights, then looked down and did her brother's shy-smile thing. A few measures into the next song she stopped abruptly. She stared at the mike as if she'd lost her place, then looked toward me and laughed. "Excuse me, everyone," she said. Aerin set her guitar on the stand and walked to my table. She rubbed the yellow hat as we hugged. "Don't go anywhere," she whispered. "Don't disappear on me."

When she'd settled again behind the mike she said, "That was my long-lost cousin, Hanna Callahan. We used to be professional cha-cha dancers. This song's for her."

"Butter Girl Blues" rocked the house. After a few more solo numbers, she was joined by three of the guys from Fish Bowl. She set aside the guitar, moved to the piano, and that's when she really took off. No more shy smiling and downcast eyes; with other musicians to work with, Aerin soared.

She closed with a beautiful solo cover of "Hometown," Chinook's first hit. When the applause faded and she'd walked offstage, I turned to a guy sitting at the table next to mine. "She looks happy," I said.

He eyed me like I was nuts. "Why wouldn't she be?"

I settled back, nodding.

><

I got a message to join her backstage. She was sitting on a lopsided three-legged couch talking to the Fish Bowl drummer in a small smoky room. She jumped up and hugged me. "I can't believe I spotted you," she said. "Usually I'm in such a zone. Must have been the hat." She rubbed it again and turned to the drummer. "It was Will's. He gave it to her after she broke his heart." She put her arms on my shoulders. "I can leave in a bit. Let's get something to eat and I'll tell you all about him. He's nineteen now, by the way."

The drummer stubbed out a smoke. "I'll let you two catch up. You're still going to join us for the Big Joe Williams medley, right?"

Aerin said, "I'll be there."

Once we were alone I said, "Does the band know who you are?"

She nodded. "Some of them used to back up Chinook."

"Do you always perform as Sylvia Callahan?"

"I hardly perform at all, Hanna. But I'm writing and arranging a lot for others and when I have stuff I want to try out with an audience, I put on the name and play someplace where I have friends. What are you doing in Chicago, for heaven's sake?"

I dropped my coat on a table. Fish Bowl had just taken the stage. Applause gave way to loud guitars. "It's a really long story. Do you need a place to stay? I live alone; you could crash with me."

"Maybe I will, thanks. The train got in too late for me to get a hotel room before the gig and I had to come straight to the club. Sam, the drummer, said I could stay at his place, but it might be less complicated at yours."

"Less complicated?"

"A couple years ago he and I had a thing. He just got married and his wife . . ." She rocked her head from side to side. "She doesn't love me."

"Then crash with me. So tell me about Beth. Tell me about your parents. Tell me about *you*."

She raised an eyebrow. "You skipped someone. But maybe there's a reason you did. Are you with anyone?"

I shook my head. "There've been a few two-month mistakes, but no, I'm not with anyone."

"Two-month mistakes," she murmured. Her eyes lost focus and she dropped inside her head. "Nice way to put it." She resurfaced. "Beth's married."

"A lawyer?"

"A cellist. I introduced them. She resisted the setup for over a year but I persevered. It was getting ridiculous; someone had to do something. Beth was queen of the two-month mistakes. She and Matt are so happy; it's usually fun to be around them. Now would you answer my question: Why Chicago?" My sigh was so long and loud, she dropped back onto the sofa laughing. "Sit down and talk."

We crammed four years into twenty minutes. I told her about hating art school and dropping out after a year and starting over at DePaul in stage design. She told me about living in New York for a while, followed by a year in Tucson.

"You disappeared," she said. "When I got back to Minneapolis that summer, I went to your house a couple of times, but no one was there. E-mail bounced back, and you'd taken down your website."

"After graduation I took a road trip with some friends for a few weeks, then Mom and I spent the rest of the summer in Maine. In September I went off to college in Rhode Island. After that school year she quit Whipple and followed her boyfriend to Canada. They live there permanently now, so that's where I go when I'm on break."

"You couldn't even drop a postcard?"

"That was a crazy winter, Aerin. I guess I wanted to move on."

She focused on a distant place. "That happens. I moved on pretty quickly myself. Not long after that strange scene with the old woman, I knew I had to get out of Minneapolis and change things and try being on my own. I was so dependent on my family propping me up. I went to Tucson, then decided to move to New York. It was a good move. I fell in love a couple of times, studied with some terrific musicians, wrote a lot of songs. One January I got tired of the snow and moved to Arizona for a while. Now I'm back in Minneapolis. I got my GED last month, and I've even bought a house. Lots of changes, but I guess I don't need to tell you anything about that. I can't believe you've totally given up drawing, Hanna. Your work was so good."

"I haven't given anything up—I still take classes and paint as much as I can on my own when I have time. And if you thought I was good before, you should see some of my new things. I've just refocused, that's all."

"But why? What happened?"

"Nothing, really. Art school was all about egos. I needed to get out."

"And theater's different? That's hard to believe."

"Of course not, but it's . . ." I looked down at my hands and saw faint red traces of paint in the roughened skin and the scar where a saw had slipped across my palm last summer. "Like tonight, when the band joined you on stage—it's sort of like that."

"Sort of like how?" She narrowed her eyes, but from the smile on her face I could tell she knew.

I shrugged. "At least for now, it's a lot more fun playing with others." I shoved my hands into the pockets of my coat. "Did your dad ever try getting in touch with that woman?"

She dropped her head back on the couch. "He called her a few times, but she wouldn't talk. She died a couple of years ago."

"The photo?"

She nodded. "Her friend sent it to him. Is your mother still teaching?"

"She's working very happily in a yarn shop. She's crazy in love."

Aerin stretched out her legs and closed her eyes. "Do you think, Hanna, that true love is required for a happy ending?"

I laughed. "I think, Aerin, that we're both too young to be thinking about any ending at all."

As soon as she'd finished her number with the band, she packed up her guitar, grabbed a small duffel bag, and we headed out into the storm.

We slogged silently through snow that had drifted into knee-deep piles. A corner store two blocks from my apartment was open and doing a brisk blizzard business. I motioned her in. The way the storm was raging, I suspected she'd be camped out with me for more than one night. I needed to make sure we didn't starve.

She started filling out numbers for a lottery ticket. I went to the cooler for milk and orange juice. By the time I paid for the groceries, she'd disappeared.

I found her outside the store. The guitar case and duffel were lying on the bench in a bus shelter. She was kicking snow into the air. She held a phone to her ear. "I'm calling Will. He's in college in California, did I mention that? Got a baseball scholarship to USC."

I moaned. "Aerin, please, no."

She shook her head. "You two have unfinished business and you have to face him sometime, you know that. You want to, anyway. Admit it. Hold on. Dang. It's his voice mail." She listened to his spiel before shoving the phone at me. "Say hi."

"Aerin, grow up."

She grinned. "After you say hi."

I spoke into the phone. "Hi, Will."

She pulled the phone back. "Hey, little brother, can you guess who that was? Call when you get this. Well, call if it's not too late. Don't forget the time difference for once, okay? It's about ten forty-five here in Chicago and I'm standing on a street corner in the middle of a blizzard. So—did you guess who that was that said hi? I ran into her tonight at the gig. Here's a hint: She still has your yellow hat."

>✦<

The radiator hissed when we entered the apartment. I heard the sound of paws hitting the kitchen floor.

"A cat!" Aerin said happily as she spotted it slinking guiltily along a wall. "I've been thinking about getting one. What's its name?"

I didn't answer.

"Cat got your tongue?" she said, laughing. Before I could reply, her phone rang.

I opened the closet to hang up our coats. Please, I thought, don't let it be Will.

"Will!" she cried. "You got my message. . . . Yeah, I know, it's incredible. I was doing this white-hot set and there she was sitting in the room and she was wearing your hat. I'm crashing at her place. It's a cool apartment. Lots of paintings. And she has a cat but she won't tell me its name. She dropped out of art school years ago. Here, you talk to her."

I shook my head. She jiggled the phone. "You know you want to. At least say hi."

I did want to say hi, but I was more than a little bit scared about what might happen next.

"She looks frightened," Aerin said to him. "So be sweet."

I took the phone. "Hey, Will."

"Hanna! This is great. Kind of weird, though, because Mom and I were just talking about you the other night and then suddenly Aerin finds you and—"

"Will, slow down. Hold on a sec." I pressed the phone

to my chest as I stared at Aerin sternly. "You don't need to smirk."

"I must be a hopeless romantic."

"You're a hopeless something. If you need to use the bathroom, it's that way. The tub's clean if you feel like a good soak. You can sleep on the futon. Blankets and pillows are in the bedroom closet."

"Got any Cheerios?"

"They're in the cupboard by the stove. Would you mind putting away the milk and juice?"

"What a hostess." She picked up the grocery bag and walked to the kitchen.

"And by the way," I called to her as I settled into a chair, getting comfortable for what I suddenly hoped would be a very long phone call, "the cat's name is Jailbait."